ADVANCE PRAISE FOR

"Eddie will win your heart."

—Vaunda Micheaux Nelson, author of *No Crystal Stair*

"Veteran author Lois Ruby's cleverly constructed mystery combines robberies and robotics, baseball and bar mitzvahs, quirky characters and abundant humor, into one enormously enjoyable story. Never has a community service project produced more comic, creepy, calamitous, and (in the end) completely satisfying results than Eddie's stint at Silver Brook. Hooray for Eddie Whatever!"

—Claudia Mills, author of *The Lost Language* and *Zero Tolerance*

"Once again, Lois Ruby delivers a story middle-grade readers will relish!"

—Doris Baker, Publisher, Filter Press, LLC

"Lois Ruby's storytelling is at its finest, carefully balancing hilarious action scenes and fast-paced plot twists. Ruby skillfully explores Eddie's worries about his family's financial problems and the tragedies of Jewish history, without ever becoming too heavy. The voices of the characters ring true and hit all the right notes. Middle-school readers will identify with Eddie as he races to catch a criminal, build a robot, and maybe even connect with his first crush, all while learning what kind of person he really wants to be."

—Susannah Levine, library media specialist,
Andover Middle School, Andover, KS

EDDIE Whatever

LOIS RUBY

CAROLRHODA BOOKS
MINNEAPOLIS

Carolrhoda Books®
An imprint of Lerner Publishing Group, Inc.
241 First Avenue North
Minneapolis, MN 55401 USA

For reading levels and more information, look up this title at www.lernerbooks.com.

Main body text set in Bembo Std.
Typeface provided by Monotype Typography.

Library of Congress Cataloging-in-Publication Data

Names: Ruby, Lois, author.
Title: Eddie Whatever / Lois Ruby.
Description: Minneapolis : Carolrhoda Books, [2021] | Audience: Ages 9–12. |
    Audience: Grades 4–6. | Summary: Thirteen-year-old Eddie's Mitzvah Project takes
    him to Silver Brook retirement home, where his assumptions about the elderly are
    upended by a ghost, a thief, long-running disagreements, and unexpected romance.
Identifiers: LCCN 2020012561 (print) | LCCN 2020012562 (ebook) |
    ISBN 9781541579187 | ISBN 9781728417417 (ebook)
Subjects: CYAC: Old age—Fiction. | Nursing homes—Fiction. | Voluntarism—
    Fiction. | Bar mitzvah—Fiction. | Jews—United States—Fiction. | Family life—
    Fiction.
Classification: LCC PZ7.R8314 Edd 2021 (print) | LCC PZ7.R8314 (ebook) | DDC
    [Fic]—dc23

LC record available at https://lccn.loc.gov/2020012561
LC ebook record available at https://lccn.loc.gov/2020012562

Manufactured in the United States of America
1-47187-47904-6/2/2021

Evan Charles Ruby,
as promised, this one's for you!

1

How does Mom find it crumpled in the bottom of my backpack, where it's been sitting for the past three weeks? She pulls the letter out and irons it with her palms. "Did you read this, Eddie? It says all the bar and bat mitzvah students have to choose a mitzvah project. What a terrific idea!"

I grab my baseball pants out of the dryer and shake out the wrinkles. You can hardly see the grass stains, though the hole in the seat could be humiliating after another couple of slides into second. The jersey thuds to my knees—No. 5, Hank Greenberg's number, because back in his day, the '30s and '40s, my hero was called the Hebrew Hammer.

"Ugh, do I have to? Can't you just call Rabbi Kefler and tell him I'm—"

"Edward Benjamin Lewin." Trouble, when she calls me by my full name. "You'd better get on board with this quickly, because you need to put in a minimum of twenty-five hours over the next three months."

"Twenty-five hours! When? I have regular school and Hebrew school, b'nai mitzvah class on Tuesdays, baseball on Thursdays, Robotics Club Wednesday mornings, synagogue Saturday mornings. Tell me when I can fit in a mitzvah project."

"Monday and Wednesday afternoons, and I've got just the place. I saw in the paper the other day that Silver Brook Pavilion welcomes volunteers."

I've heard of it. Tessa Schwartz in my b'nai mitzvah class decided to volunteer there but quit practically immediately. What a recommendation.

Mom's already grabbed her tablet and pulled up the website for the retirement home. *"Silver Brook is a continuum-of-care facility for senior citizens—lovable old folks who are thrilled to have young people around.* See?"

She shows me the home page on the tablet screen.

SILVER BROOK PAVILION
WHERE OLD IS THE NEW YOUNG

Are they kidding? I picture shrunken crones licking lollipops or blowing pinwheels. Baldies playing hit and catch with a Nerf bat and ball, rock-paper-scissors to decide who bats first.

"And you can walk there, perfect. You can start next Monday. We'll call the administrator to set it up."

"Aw, Mom, gimme a break."

Instead she gives me her famous evil eye while looking up the number. My mom: when she decides something, an army of fire ants under her bare feet wouldn't change her mind.

After school on Monday, Mom marches me to the old folks' place and deserts me at the main entrance.

I think about making one last bid for freedom, but she's got *that look* on her face, so I whoosh in my breath and blow out a gust of hot air as I tromp up the wheelchair ramp to my doom.

Despite Silver Brook's slogan, there's nothing young about the wrinkly people lining the building's front porch. They make Grandma and Grandpa in Cincinnati look like high schoolers. Some lean their chins on canes. Others look stuck in wheelchairs or rocking chairs, or they're backed onto their walker seats. All of 'em look like they're watching a silent movie playing in midair. At least until every pair of eyes rotates toward me.

One woman points at me with a skinny, unlit cigar stuck in a plastic holder. "Who's this?" she croaks. I mean, she doesn't *croak*, as in die on the spot, but she sounds like a bullfrog, and her brown face is as worn and cracked as Dad's briefcase. The fancy gold watch that's slid down from her wrist to her elbow catches a glint of sunlight and almost blinds me.

The lady next to her pulls thick glasses down from her halo of cloud-white hair and googly-eyes me. "Could be Mrs. Goldfarb's youngest great-grandson. See the way his hair hangs in his eyes?"

I swipe my hand across my forehead, but my squirrel-colored hair just flops right back. Two guys who've been smoking cigars, blowing fruity puffs into each other's faces, turn to stare. One of them hooks his cane around my arm and reels me in.

"Afternoon, sonny. Watcha up to?"

"Leave him alone, Herman!" the other cigar man barks.

"Mind your own p's and q's, Maurie." Cigar smoke blasts out of Herman.

"I'm Eddie Lewin," I say. "The new volunteer."

"Herman Stark," says the cigar man who lassoed me with his cane. "And this nudnik here is Maurie Glosser."

"I'm capable of introducing myself, you old flea-bag. Some of us still have our memories intact, you know."

"Don't mind them," says the cigar lady with the elegant watch. "I'm Ethylene Callahan, and this is Rosa Dorian."

"Nice to meet you all." When I take a step back to extricate my arm from the crook of Mr. Stark's cane, the automatic door swooshes open.

Inside, two women in wheelchairs guard the lobby like the fierce stone lions I saw last summer at the New York Public Library. One lady has red knee socks pulled up on her skinny legs. No old-lady shoes. Her straight, straw-like hair hangs to her shoulders, the color of a bruised lemon. The other lady—who's shrunk down to the size of a fifth grader—is covered in purple, head to toe, including purple blotches on her hands. Her smile flashes off and on, reminding me of a changing stoplight.

With a face twisted into a frown, the lady with the red socks leans toward me. "Welcome to Silver

Brook." *Velcome*. Her accent's barely noticeable, but there. "Call me Lina. Everyone calls me that except *her*. I'm a twin, you know."

How would I know? And who is *her*? "My name's Eddie L—"

"Whatever. I'll forget it in two minutes. How long's your sentence with us?"

Great start. Mom promised Silver Brook an hour every Monday and Wednesday. In an hour you can play four innings or three video games. But here? Only fifty-five minutes to go. "I'm here till June."

Lina says, "You must be one of the mitzvah project kids."

"Yeah," I say with a sigh. "My bar mitzvah is barely three months off. The whole family's flying into Oklahoma City for it. But I'll be a no-show unless I do my twenty-five hours of community service. Believe me, I'd rather be messing around with the robot that my squad's building at school or hitting baseballs out of the park." Like *that* ever happens.

Lina leans forward again, stretching a long neck, and drills her milky-blue eyes into me. "Baseball, huh?"

"Yep. Proud to play for the Oakridge Oilers." Which is famous statewide for being second from the bottom of all the Oklahoma middle schools. At least we aren't *the* bottom-feeders.

"Hmm. You might be an improvement over the usual boring kids we get here." In her next breath, she ruins the whole thing: "You're short for thirteen. Tuck in your shirt, kid."

I jam my knee-length Oilers jersey into my jeans, so it looks like a blown-out rubber tire around my middle.

"Don't mind me," she adds. "I'm a cranky old witch."

"Aw, I'll bet you're not as cranky as you think." Said it to be polite, but I believe her.

"Oh," says the little purple lady, "she's as bitter as beet horseradish."

"And it's best not to cross me!" Lina puts up her gnarled dukes and starts punching the air. No one would believe that I'm air-sparring with an old lady in a wheelchair.

Thankfully, she lowers her fists before I accidentally sock her in the jaw. "I should warn you, Eddie Whatever."

The other lady makes a face.

Before I can ask, *Warn me about what?*, Lina says, "The place is haunted."

2

A middle-aged woman in a black business suit and some kind of ripply pinkish shirt waddles over to me on spiked heels, trailed by a super-sized poodle that prances like a merry-go-round pony. "Oh, Halina, not the haunted thing again."

"Can't deny the truth," Lina mutters. "I should know, because the ghost is my twin sister, Toibe. Pure evil, that one."

And the purple lady looks me right in the eye and says, "Oh, yes, it's quite true. There is a ghost here at Silver Brook, and she's not purple, not at all purple."

"Ladies, please." The woman closes her eyes and takes a deep breath like Mom the third time she asks me to take out the trash. When she opens them, she's smiling. "Hello. You're Eddie Lewin, aren't you?"

"Yes, ma'am, that's me."

The dog sniffs my feet and crotch and throws me a dirty look.

A hand shoots out. "Hester Brubaker. I run this haven for seniors, and this is our mascot, Flambé. We have septuagenarians, octogenarians, nonagenarians, and one well-preserved soul, Mrs. Dorian, who's a hundred and two and sharp as a tack!"

I look at her blankly.

"Oh, excuse the jargon. I mean people in their seventies, eighties, and nineties." She could have said that in the first place, but I guess she likes spouting flashy words. "Come, Flambé, let's show Eddie around so he'll feel right at home."

No way I'll ever feel *at home* in this place where everything smells like the clothes stored in our basement. And already Flambé hates me. What kind of a name is that for a dog, anyway?

I start to follow Ms. Brubaker and Flambé, but Lina grabs my knee in a stronger grip than you'd expect. "This one's mine. Buzz off, Brubaker."

"Halina, be nice to Eddie. And to me, for a change." Another deep sigh.

Sheesh, now they're in a tug-of-war. Lina won't let go of my leg, and Ms. Brubaker tries to drag me away by my best batting arm. Yeah, I'm a switch-hitter, equally rotten from both sides of the plate.

Quick, I have to choose which vital limb to sacrifice—an arm or a leg—or else be stretched like a slingshot. "Ladies, please let go. There's enough of me to go around."

Both women drop their holds, glaring at each other.

"Well, Eddie," says Ms. Brubaker, "I see you've already met the ever-charming Halina Kempinski."

Lina says, "Kid, don't be taken in by Miss Goody-Two-Shoes and her stuck-up hound from Hades."

Ms. Brubaker clicks her index fingers together. She could dig potatoes and onions out of the ground with those sharp fingernails. "Halina, you might want to freshen up for dinner."

She leads me across the lobby. "You'll hear a lot of colorful talk around here. No need to take it seriously." Tapping the side of her head with one of those bright-red, pointy nails, she adds, "Some of our residents are a bit, well, *unique*, but we love each and every one of them. Don't we?" She says this last part to a woman in scrubs pushing a cart full of pills. "Lupita, meet our new volunteer, Eddie Lewin. Lupita's our incomparable charge nurse, who's been with us since Silver Brook opened four years ago."

"Welcome." Lupita waves an elbow at me, keeping both hands on the clattering cart.

"And there's Judy, our receptionist." Flambé trots behind the counter and noses Judy, who doesn't look up from her computer screen. Her fingers fly across a keyboard while a phone's propped between her shoulder and her chin. "How's it going, sweetie?" she mouths, her ear to the phone.

"Come, Flambé." Ms. Brubaker points down a tan hallway, straight as a bowling lane. "That way to the residents' apartments and the elevator. On the second floor we have our crafts studio, our library, and our fitness center—the domain of our occupational therapist, Clara. You'll meet her later. The dayroom's here, computer lab across the hall."

I peek inside as we pass it. One iMac. A lab?

"Dining hall farther down this way. And from here you can see . . ."

Ms. Brubaker leads me to a huge window. "Our lovely back patio, overlooking our garden and our pond! Of course, it's fenced in for the security of our residents."

In case any residents try to escape, which I'd like to do right now.

"Those two geese in the pond are a couple. They mate for life, you know."

While I'm checking out the married geese, Ms. Brubaker does a sudden about-face, nearly tripping over Flambé, who's not as quick on his feet. "Oh, meet the Goldfarbs, the sweetest couple. They're our newest residents."

Mr. and Mrs. Goldfarb keep perfect pace with each other, pushing their side-by-side matching walkers down the hall.

"Ruth and Sidney, this is Eddie Lewin, a volunteer."

Mrs. Goldfarb smiles with a big mouthful of teeth that I bet aren't her starter set. She pokes her husband's arm. "Why, look, darling, it's a bar mitzvah boy!" Nothing registers on Mr. Goldfarb's face, or in his eyes. He doesn't open his mouth, but his wife says, "What? No, this is Monday. We'll have dinner at Miriam's on Thursday, three more nights." She sees the puzzled look on my face. "Oh, you're confused, aren't you, Eddie, dear? You see, Sidney and I have been married for sixty-eight years. I know exactly what he'd say, if he could. After the stroke, well . . ."

"We'll talk more later, Ruth." Ms. Brubaker pulls me toward a broad-shouldered, brown-skinned man with jingling keys clipped to his belt loops. "Eddie, this is Hank Fridell, in charge of maintenance. He fixes everything around here, even a broken heart or two. Hank's a favorite with our young volunteers. He has five little Fridellies at home—imagine! I, myself, am childless."

My hand disappears into Hank's ping-pong-paddle-sized one.

"Pleased to have young folks here," he says, scratching Flambé behind his ears with his free hand. "Anything you need, or anything the residents ask you about, feel free to come to me."

Should I say it? "Actually, Mr. Fridell, I hear there's a mischievous spirit loose in this place."

"Call me Hank, son. You bet, Miss Lina and Mrs. DiAngelo keep talking about that ghostie spirit thing. I just listen."

Ms. Brubaker throws her hands up in the air. "Stop encouraging those women. Right, Flambé?"

The dog thinks about it and has no comment, but I catch a smile playing on Hank's face.

"I'm sure I'll see you around, Eddie," he says. "Gotta run right now, though. This is my day job. I teach math at the junior college Mondays and Thursdays. Five kids, like Ms. Brubaker said, that's a lot of meat and potatoes to put on the table. By the way, ma'am, Mrs. Dorian's commode backed up again. She must still be throwing in paper-towel wads. Want me to call the plumber before I go?"

"I'll take care of it, Hank."

I sneak a look at the time on my phone; must have stopped. Still forty-seven minutes to go, and twenty-four more hours after that.

3

"Any questions so far, Eddie?" Ms. Brubaker asks as we step out of the elevator and head to the fitness center on the second floor.

"Um . . ." I feel like I should be able to think of something, but my mind's blank. "I was wondering how your dog got his name." Flambé stares at me like he's insulted to be called a dog.

"Obviously, he's a French poodle. In his native tongue, his name means *flaming*. Note the reddish hair on his chin and paws. Highly rare in a poodle. Hence, Flambé." The dog wags his stub of a tail to brag.

"Oh, look, Mrs. Perlmuter is just starting her yoga class! Let's join in, shall we? Flambé, sit!"

He doesn't. He admires his hairy body in the mirror that lines one wall, then inspects the bars and bikes and dumbbells scattered around the rest of the room.

"Flambé, come!" He saunters over and ducks as Ms. Brubaker kicks off her heels and falls in line next to a seventy-something man in floppy shorts held up with wide suspenders. You'd think he'd at least wear long pants to cover up those ropy blue veins trailing all the way up both legs.

"Earl Archer, this is Eddie, our new volunteer."

The old man gives me the once-over. "Needs some meat on his bones."

Ms. Brubaker goes into flamingo mode. "Did you know that flamingos can sleep on one leg this way? Try it, Eddie."

It's harder than it looks, but maybe it will help me throw to second, even third, without falling on my face. I'd rather not smash my face like a pumpkin before my bar mitzvah, so I keep trying the flamingo thing and feel ridiculous.

The yoga teacher, Mrs. Perlmuter, must be at least ninety, but she can twist like a pretzel. Earl and the three other people in the class struggle to keep up with her.

"Breathe from deeeeeep within your soul," Mrs. Perlmuter croons, her eyes closed.

We try, even the one who's dragging an oxygen machine along with her.

All I can think is, *I am NEVER getting old!*

Ms. Brubaker easily switches legs. "You know Tessa Schwartz, don't you? She volunteered last month."

Do I have to blush just because she mentioned Tessa? "She goes to my school, and we're in the b'nai mitzvah class together." I lean against the wall to switch legs.

Ms. Brubaker stretches her arms out, ready to take off into the wild blue. With a heavy breeze, she'll hit the ceiling. "Well, the child quit after two weeks. Don't quit on us, Eddie. It does not look good on your college application."

Which is four or five years off. I'll still have plenty of time to save my reputation if I bail on day one at Silver Brook. Tempting.

"But, Ms. Brubaker, what exactly am I supposed to *do* here?"

Ms. Brubaker slips her shoes back on and leads me back out into the hall. "Oh, freshen people's water pitchers. Prop up their chair pillows. Push wheelchairs. Help out in the computer lab."

We're in the elevator again, on our way back to the main floor. "More important, what do you *not* do?" She begins ticking off the list. "Don't lift anybody or help them out of bed. Don't give anybody food or meds. Don't help them to the bathroom."

Ewww, never!

"Don't take tips from them. Don't open windows. When in doubt, find Lupita or Hank." I notice she doesn't suggest finding *her*.

The elevator door dings open. Ms. Brubaker breezes across the lobby to Judy's desk, grabs a stapled packet of papers, and hands them to me. "Here's our volunteer handbook. It's all fairly intuitive. You'll find your groove. Most important, be cheerful! Everyone here at Silver Brook needs a bright, smiley face." She flashes me a fake smile that doesn't work its way to her beady, dark eyes.

With a glance at her watch, which is roughly the diameter of a hubcap, Ms. Brubaker says, "Now you'll have to excuse me. Flambé and I have a vital staffing meeting. We're worried about Mrs. Boniface, who's been ultra-gloomy lately. No one's come to visit the poor thing in two years. Anyway, make yourself at home, Eddie. Get to know our residents."

Flambé throws me a toothy sneer over his shoulder and prances away with her, so I tuck the handbook under my arm and head over to Lina, who's slumped at her sentry post. The purple lady's gone.

"Excuse me, Mrs. Kempinski . . ."

"Missus? Hah! You'd never catch me trotting down the aisle. I told you, it's just Lina."

"Right. Lina. What did you mean about Silver Brook being haunted . . . by your sister?"

"Not just sister. *Twin.* Here's an example. Last night I'd barely fluffed my pillow when my bedside clock started flashing midnight."

Electrical short. My little sister, Gabby, always lectures me about electricity, since she's gonna be an electrical engineer in about twenty years.

Lina spins a wheelie in her chair. "But that's not the worst of it." With a crooked finger, she motions for me to squat down so she can whisper in my ear. "She talks to me from the heating vent. Not in her own voice, of course."

Oh, come on. But I humor her because, hey, I have grandparents. Lina's probably a good twenty years older than they are, but the basic steps still apply: listen, answer their questions with more than a grunt, and assure them you're getting enough to eat. "What does she say, Lina?"

"She says, *It's time you gave it all up—tossed in the towel, bit the dust, bought the farm.*"

Sheesh, that's brutal.

A bell tinkles over the PA system. Lina spins another wheelie, and people start streaming through the lobby, pushing walkers, racing canes, rolling wheels, and weaving in and out as if they're in a slo-mo relay race.

A fire drill? What to do in a senior citizens' home in a fire drill? They can't all rush outside and stand by the flagpole like at school.

Lina nearly knocks me over in the rush to get in line, so I follow.

"Where are we going?"

"You got a watch? Oh, that's right, your generation doesn't know how to tell time. Well, take out your phone, and you'll see it's four thirty. Dinnertime."

In my world, four thirty is after-school snack time, or batting practice time, or Hebrew school time, or time for Star Trek *TNG* reruns, but it definitely isn't dinnertime.

I plant myself like a statue in the middle of the lobby as the whole parade streams by slowly, complaining about the crummy food they can't wait to sink their teeth (or gums) into. The sign outside the dining hall says today's meal is smothered steak and smashed potatoes and chopped salad. Sounds like the murderous work of a sinister chef.

Along comes Maurie with a walking stick in each hand. "Did you see the menu? Holy Moses, it's that shoe leather they pass off as steak. I'm in the mood for spaghetti, but do you think they asked me?"

Lina says, "You're lucky you get any food, so stop grousing, old man."

Maurie bends down and whispers in my ear, "She's older than I am. Older than dirt, that one." He ambles into the dining hall, and I guess I'm supposed to follow him and see what I can do to help the staff.

Can't wait to get home to *real* dinner.

4

At home, food's on the table—chicken tacos with fake cheese, spicy rice, and salad (not chopped). Mom sets down the salsa bowl and flashes me one of those way-too-eager looks. "So, how was your first day at Silver Brook?"

I make the usual full-blooded report: "Okay."

"Details, that's what mothers live for."

"Mom!" cries Gabby. "You're interrogating him."

Dad doesn't look up from the taco collapsed on his plate.

"You okay, Dad?" I ask.

"Yeah, sure, Eddie," he says glumly, and Mom averts her eyes. Something's up. Gabby and I exchange *who knows* shrugs.

"Can I go ice skating with Olivia on Saturday?" Gabby begs. "Please, please, please."

"Sunday, yes. Saturday, no." Mom crunches into a taco to signal that the subject is closed.

Gabby wails, "I never get to do fun stuff like *normal* fifth graders do."

"At least you don't have to be a flamingo while a ninety-year-old lady trots around in lime-colored tights," I say, "or listen to someone rant about weird stuff like . . . like . . ."

Dad snaps off a chunk of carrot from his salad and pushes the rest of his plate away. "Like what?"

"Like ghosts. A couple of wacky ladies say Silver Brook is haunted."

That gets Dad's full attention. "Ridiculous."

"I know, but they think so."

Gabby's taco dribbles meat over her plate. "We're all made of electrical energy."

Mom gives her *that look*. "Don't talk with your mouth full, honey."

After a gulpy swallow, Gabby continues. "Did you ever hear of battery drain? Some people say ghosts feed on our energy, or the energy in our phones or flashlights, to pump themselves up. Cool, isn't it?"

Dad mutters, "Cool, but hogwash."

What's with him? Gabby and I flash eye rolls

across the table. The cool thing about having a sister is that you never really have to *talk* to her.

Tuesday afternoon at the synagogue. The five of us next-ups for bar or bat mitzvah are bunched around the front end of the conference table, with Rabbi Kefler parked at the head.

My prayer book stands tall in front of me, shielding my phone so I can text Tessa (Hebrew name Tamar) across the table.

Me: Why did you quit the old folks place?

She lifts her head, with its wild, curly black mop of hair, and winks at me. *Winks at me!* Her hands drop to her lap.

Tessa: tell you later

Me: a hint?

"Eliahu?"

Tessa: long story

"Eliahu!"

My head shoots up. My Hebrew name sounds sharp on the rabbi's tongue.

He reaches across Joe (Yosef) to tap a long finger on my phone. "All right, people, I give all of you five seconds to stash your phones out of reach or they go in my impressive collection."

There's a frantic scurrying around of phones finding pockets.

"So, Eliahu, would you and Tamar care to share your conversation?"

Deep breath. "We were talking about our mitzvah projects." Sort of true.

"Good, let's discuss how they're coming along. Shmuel, I believe you're working at the food bank?"

Sam, such a show-off, jumps up at attention to give his smug report. "I've personally shelved about six tons of canned goods, including—excuse me, Rabbi—including pork and beans."

"Don't judge," Rabbi Kefler says dismissively. "Adina?"

She's the only one whose Hebrew name is also her regular name. "I've been walking therapy dogs for three disabled people. That's a lot of poop to clean up."

Over our laughs, Rabbi says, "Eliahu, tell us about your mitzvah project."

"Silver Brook Pavilion," I mutter, "where old is the new young."

Rabbi Kefler brightens. He sees hope for me after all. "Ah, yes! I visit members of our congregation at Silver Brook. Tamar, weren't you volunteering there too? You've run into Halina Kempinski, no doubt?"

Tessa pipes up, "Is she totally on another planet, or what?"

"Not totally, not even mostly," Rabbi Kefler assures us.

"Which part isn't?" I ask. "She says the place is haunted by her twin sister." Across the table, Tessa's eyes flash some sort of message. I can always read Gabby's eyes, but Tessa's are harder.

Rabbi Kefler glances from Tessa to me and rearranges the skullcap that covers the bald spot in the middle of his blond curls. "So, let this be our pithy thought for the day. Take it from Richard Slavin, a man who became a bar mitzvah in the sixties, but who later went on to be a Buddhist monk. Interesting switch. Anyway, whatever this man's spiritual practices are, he has something important to say."

Rabbi scrolls through his phone.

"Mr. Slavin, now known as Radhanath Swami, tells us that we tend to judge others by their appearances and to find only their negative qualities.

Search beneath the surface, he says, and we discover that the faults we see might be because of trauma or abuse or heartbreak. Think about this in terms of Halina Kempinski, will you, Tamar and Eliahu? Back to business. Yosef, wake up. Top of page eighty. Read."

5

Tessa and I wait on the curb for our parents to pick us up. It's okay if it takes Mom an hour to get here. "So, why *did* you quit Silver Brook?"

"You have to swear you'll never breathe a word of it. Swear?"

I flash the Boy Scout's honor sign and also a slice across my throat to say that I'd die under extreme torture before telling, but what calls for such top security?

"You know how Lina Kempinski keeps insisting that the place is haunted?" Tessa says. "Of course, I didn't believe a word of it."

"Didn't, or don't?"

"Well, you know how hot they keep it there. You could skate around in your own sweat, and the residents are still bundled up."

"Maybe when they pass seventy they lose a lot of their insulation, like our attic did."

"So, there I am in Lina's room helping her get ready for a nap. I bring the glass for her to put her teeth in and spray her handkerchief with that stinky rosewater that she likes to sniff as she falls asleep."

"And then?" I wonder if she heard someone talking through the heating vent.

"Here's the creepy part. The temperature dropped from ninety degrees to freezing. I mean, teeth-chattering cold! In two minutes from sweating like a camel to icicles on my tonsils. You do know what they say about ghosts, don't you?"

"Nope, not an expert in that field. Make it quick—here comes my mom." Wait, it's my dad. He's usually at Crest Foods working until seven. I stick my head in the window. "Hey, Dad, could you hold on a sec?"

Tessa tells me, "It's a *thing* in ghostly lore that the temperature totally plummets when a ghost passes. I saw a YouTube about it. Anyway, Lina's room freaked me out. That's why I quit."

"Gotta be some explanation besides Toibe the Ghost. My sister, Gabby, would say there was an electrical failure in Lina's room. Or else the AC kicked on suddenly. Come back to Silver Brook, and we can check it out together."

"Nah, I've got other priorities. And like we were just saying, some of the people there are kind of . . . a lot."

"I know, but think about that Swami guy who says you've got to look past the surface."

"Hm. I guess. I mean, if you didn't know me, you might think I was a wild child raised by feral pigs."

I grin. "Aren't you?"

"Possibly, with this hair. There's enough to cover a small black bear." *A beautiful black bear*, I'm thinking.

"Or stuff a couch cushion," I suggest. Wait, does that sound creepy? This little *tick-tick* thing is happening in my chest, like I ate a radioactive Skittle. It suddenly occurs to me: Tessa is not just Tessa. She's a *girl*.

"Your dad's waving."

"Right. See you later." I climb into the car. The AC's cranked up meat-locker high, typical of a guy who spends his days in fruits and veggies at the grocery store. I remember what Tessa said about temperature drops. But just because it's cold enough to preserve a fresh side of beef in the car doesn't mean a ghostly passenger lurks in the back seat.

To be sure, I turn around to inspect. Only thing back there is a net bag of clementines—no see-through figure slithering in through the cracked window to juggle those golf-ball-sized oranges.

At Robotics Club on Wednesday morning, we're pushing to get Bunko ready for regionals in June. Our sponsor, Ms. Perini, is a wreck. She's developed a tic—always winking as though there's a hair in her eye. Joe and Azmara and I huddle over our robot while Ms. Perini stalks across the lab, chewing on her cuticles.

Azmara studies Bunko from all angles. "He looks too much like one of those old Minions, all ovoid and googly-eyed. We should soften him, make him look more human."

"He's a robot! He's not supposed to look human," Joe protests.

Bunko's programmed to glide across the floor, bend over without smashing his face and denting his flimsy body, use his pincher fingers to pick up Legos, and drop them into a bucket. Easy peasy, right? Not if you're a two-foot-tall tin-can robot built by rank amateurs.

Joe bellies on the floor, examining the space between Bunko's chubby body and his turned-out feet. We built him to be steady and balanced, but he wobbles and scatters Legos.

"One thing works well—his sounds," Azmara points out.

Agreed. Every time Bunko bends over and falls on his nose or misses picking up a Lego, which is every time he tries, he whimpers pathetically.

Joe says, "It's like he's ashamed to let us down."

"He should be!" Azmara exclaims, adjusting her headscarf.

The sonic blast that's the first-period warning bell knocks Bunko over. We snatch up our backpacks as Ms. Perini locks Bunko away in the closet. You'd think he'd squawk in protest, but maybe he's glad to be rid of us for a few days.

"Back to square one," Ms. Perini tells us. "We've only got about forty school days until the competition, and I'm not going to let you mortify me at regionals. From now on, we're meeting twice a week."

Groans, protests, rebellion!

"Ah-ah!" She stares us down. "Friday. Seven a.m., sharp. Be here, kiddos, even if your parents have to carry you in on stretchers."

I actually show up for my second day at Silver Brook. Not because I'm excited about spending time here or anything. But I might want to stick around for a while and see if I can convince Tessa to come back here.

The weather's gloomy, so nobody's hanging out on the porch. No welcoming committee in the lobby either. I pass the reception desk, where Judy's busy chatting with the security guard, and head to the dayroom. A snarky argument is raging between Herman Stark and Maurie Glosser, who are parked at a table with a deck of oversized cards.

Waving a fist so that I can clearly see the cards he's holding, Maurie says, "I tell you, it was 1948."

"Idiot. It was 1949, the year Franny got stuck in a silo over in Perkins. Definitely 1949."

Herman turns his dark eyes to me. "You settle it, sonny—1948, right?"

Both men glare at me with high hopes. No idea what they're arguing about, but so what? "Mr. Glosser, Mr. Stark, I've thought about this a lot, and I'm absolutely sure it was 1950."

Herman smirks. "Didn't I tell you, Maurie? It was 1950. Hey, son, whatever your name is—"

"Eddie."

"Yeah, whatever. You know how Ethylene Callahan always wears her husband's gold watch up over her elbow?"

Mrs. Callahan is the other cigar smoker I met on Monday. "Sure, I noticed that."

"Well, guess what? She took it off when she went to sleep last night, and this morning, *pfft*, gone."

"Seriously? That's awful."

"We got a kleptomaniac living right here among us!" Maurie says.

Before I can slip into the one-iMac lab and Google what kind of maniac that is, Lina rolls by.

"It's her—Toibe. She watches to see what you love most, and that's what she takes."

"Aw, Lina, give it up!" Maurie grumbles.

"You'll see!" she threatens as she coasts down the hall.

The purple lady, whose real name is Carmina

DiAngelo, pokes her head into the dayroom. She's got a stack of photo albums balanced precariously on her lap.

"Hey, Mrs. DiAngelo. Can I talk to you for a minute?"

"Of course, dear boy. You remind me so much of my Antony. He was exquisitely purple to his dying day."

Was she married to an eggplant? "The other day, you said you believed there was someone haunting this place."

"Yes, no question."

"You've actually *seen* a ghost?"

"Heavens no! She's much too wily to let herself be seen. But I've felt her slide past me. She chilled me to the bone, she did. And she steals things."

"Do you think the ghost took Mrs. Callahan's husband's gold watch?"

The little lady pulls her eyebrows together in confusion, but after a moment she seems to get it. "Oh, I see what you're saying, dear boy. Yes, truly the ghost steals things, but not things you can hold in your hand. The most important thing of all."

She probably doesn't mean vintage baseball cards. "What's that?"

"Memory. My Antony went on to the next world in 1973. Yesterday I remembered what color eyes he had. Mahogany brown, I think . . . but today, I'm not so sure. That ghost steals our memories."

Oh, man, no way to answer that, so I switch the subject. "Could you show me some pictures in your albums?"

That brightens her up, mostly because it immediately reminds her of the exact color of her husband's eyes. (Not purple.)

When I help her return the albums to her apartment, I catch sight of an unfamiliar face through the open door of another apartment.

"That's Thelma Boniface," whispers Mrs. DiAngelo. "She never talks to us. Never has any visitors either. Rumor has it that payment for her stay at Silver Brook comes special delivery every month, anonymous, with a local postmark. Imagine living right here in town and paying for the upkeep of someone you never come to see!"

Pretty bleak. Once I've deposited Mrs. DiAngelo and her albums in her apartment, I head back down the residential hallway.

Mrs. Boniface slumps in her wheelchair in her

doorway. Seems like she's looking for company, but she doesn't respond to my goofy grin.

"Hi, Mrs. Boniface. I'm Eddie." To save time, I've stopped bothering to say my last name. The volunteer handbook says not to ask residents how they're doing, in case the answer bums both of us out. So instead, I ask, "Can I get you anything? Ice water, a clean towel?"

She gazes at me with the saddest eyes. I wonder if she has a deep, dark secret that keeps her from talking. Or is she just too old and tired to talk? Maybe you only get a certain number of words in your lifetime, and she's spent all hers.

"Want me to take you to the dayroom?"

Not a hair moves. That's how slowly she shakes her head.

"I could read you a story. I'll be back in a sec." I run to Lupita's station down the hall and grab a chair from there, along with a sappy romance novel one of the nurses left. I plant myself on the chair in the middle of the hallway, facing Mrs. Boniface, and flip to a random page: "*Rodney showed his beloved a brooch of gold lavishly encrusted with cabochon rubies, and she cried, 'Sir, do you think you can win my undying adoration so cheaply?'*"

I look up to see how she likes this pure cheesy corn. Surprise: tears are rolling down her face, dropping in big dark blobs on her dress. Should I ignore them? Or temporarily abandon her on a quest to find tissues?

Maybe she wants more action. Skipping ahead, I hit a passage where a horse pulling a carriage suddenly runs wild. With my deepest fake voice and most overblown expression, I read: *"His hooves thundered down the road, kicking up clouds of gritty dust that stung Rodney's cornflower-blue eyes. Rosalee wrestled the reins out of his hands to slow Madrigal, but the great stallion galloped with unbridled abandon, jumping hurdles and fences until, alas, he landed in a steep ravine!"*

Mrs. Boniface's face is lit up a little more, and a bunch of other people have opened their apartment doors and gotten caught up in the story. Flambé has one paw on Mrs. Boniface's foot.

"Well? Did the horse break his leg?" Maurie Glosser asks.

"Oh, Lordy, I hope they didn't have to shoot him," cries Mrs. Dorian down at the end of the hall.

Mrs. Callahan, in the doorway across from us, says, "I love a hot, juicy romance."

To which Mrs. Goldfarb next door adds, "I'll bet the sweethearts will end up under the chuppah together!"

"Weddings, that's how those cornball stories always end." Naturally, that comes from Lina, the Grinch, whose door is on the other side of the Goldfarbs' apartment.

"At our wedding, my Antony wore a purple bow tie and cummerbund . . ." Mrs. DiAngelo says before she trails off.

I finish the chapter, and my audience scatters, except for Mrs. Boniface, who's still sitting in her doorway, as lonesome as a cowboy on the prairie (except for his cows).

I gotta say *something*. "People say there's a ghost here at Silver Brook."

There's a flash in Mrs. Boniface's eyes. Fear?

"Do you like baseball, Mrs. Boniface?" Who doesn't?

An eyebrow drifts up, which I read as a yes, so I keep pitching.

"Speaking of baseball and ghosts, I heard there's a haunted hotel in Milwaukee where teams stay when they're in town to play the Brewers. Well, some of the guys swear they've had ghosts in their rooms."

Mrs. Boniface doesn't peep, but her eyes say she's listening. Progress.

"Oh, and there's a haunted hotel in St. Petersburg, Florida. Once a Red Sox pitcher was in his room there when he saw an old-fashioned man and woman flit by, which got him all tingly. So he Googled it and saw a picture of that exact couple, who'd died right there, in that hotel room, ages ago. Cool story, right? But I don't believe in ghosts. Do you?"

"Scott Williamson, that's who the Red Sox pitcher was." I turn around; Lina is right behind me. She wheels past me without another word.

6

It's a practice game against the Chickasha Chargers, but we've kept our perfect record: losses six, wins zip.

"Nice boxers." Joe points to the gigantic hole I ripped in my pants sliding into second base—a nanosecond *after* the Charger baseman had the ball in his glove. Why did I wear my old Spidey boxers today?

Coach Erdman, Joe's dad, drops me off at home, and Gabby leaps on me at the front door. "Come on, they're back there doing the whisp-whisp-whispery thing again."

With our ears pressed to Mom and Dad's door, even with my bat hearing, all I get is muffled mumbles. Until out pours one loud "JAKE LEWIN, HOW COULD YOU?" After that, there's just sniffling.

"What's going on?" Gabby asks.

I yank her into the living room and sink into the recliner, footrest boosted up grandpa-style. "They're mad at each other about something, but what?"

"They used to be so embarrassingly smoochy, even when real people were around."

I fiddle with the zapper on mute, and images flash across the TV screen—a cartoon, a preacher in a black robe, a woman warning that tornado season is in full swing. "Whatever's going on, they obviously don't want us to know about it. Aren't we a democracy? Everybody's opinion counts?"

Gabby gasps. "What if they're talking about moving to some other city? Or some altogether other *country* where there isn't good Wi-Fi or Cool Whip?"

"They couldn't move without talking to us about it. It's gotta be something else."

Gabby bolts up suddenly. "They'd better not be thinking about sending me to that genius school. I talked them out of it last year. You have to back me up on this, Eddie."

"Why is it always about you? Anyway, that wouldn't explain Dad's weird behavior or how they don't look each other in the eye. It's something worse, like, maybe one of them is sick."

Gabby considers this. "They're not coughing or

doubling over in pain, but I guess it could be some terrible disease that doesn't show, like elephantiasis."

"That shows." I toss the remote to the floor and lever myself out of the recliner.

"Nice boxers," Gabby says.

"Maybe somebody died. Grandma or Grandpa?"

"Nah, they'd tell us something that awful."

Mom comes into the living room with red eyes and a broad, sickly smile smeared across her face. "Well! I'd better start dinner!" She's as fake-bubbly as Mountain Dew. "Eddie, please light the grill outside, and Gabriella, I need you to cut up tomatoes and onions for our hamburgers." As if it took all her energy to say that little bit, Mom's shoulders sag. Maybe she is sick. Although her skin's not greenish and her eyes aren't sunken, like Mrs. Boniface's.

"What's up, Mom?" I ask, sliding the patio door open.

"Up?"

"Yeah, Gabby and I, we've noticed something's weird with you and Dad."

"I don't know what you're talking about, kids. The grill, please. Dinner's already late."

Gabby follows me to the patio, pulling the sliding door closed with a loud slap.

The flame jets up, and I slam the grill shut. "Did you notice how Mom's energy gave out, and she's asking us to do stuff *she* usually does? She's sick, I'll bet that's what it is, and Dad's coming home early to help her, picking me up at Hebrew school and stuff like that."

"Mom does look a little worn out," Gabby says. "But maybe that's just because she's been putting in extra hours on her editing for the college."

I shake my head. "They're totally hiding something. Aside from life or death stuff, what's the next-worst thing you can think of, Gab?"

She ponders for a moment. "I've got it. They're having another baby! That is so gross!"

"Eesh, they're too old. How could I tell Joe or Tessa something like that?"

"Maybe we can keep it a secret. Just say she swallowed a watermelon."

"Yeah, that'll work."

Dinner's grim. It's like somebody pressed Mute. The only noise is my teeth marching across my ear of corn, two rows at a time, then back to the left, like Mom's old typewriter.

I nearly fling my corncob across the table in shock when Dad cracks the silence: "Pass the mustard." We knock it over, all three of us reaching for it.

After a minute, Mom makes a stab at asking how school and baseball practice went, but she clearly isn't interested, so we glumly say, "Fine."

When the tension is thick enough to spread like chunky peanut butter, Gabby blurts out: "We're having a baby, aren't we?"

Mom drops her burger. Ketchup flies like blood specks. A pickle slice splatters on the tile floor.

That confirms it. She'll be a blimp by the time my bar mitzvah rolls around in June.

"A baby?" Dad's water glass earthquakes. "Why would you think that? We've got a wonderful family. Who needs a baby, especially right now?"

Especially right now? I've been hearing that a lot. What's so super important about right now besides the fact that a hair has sprouted on my chin?

"There's a lot of whispering behind closed doors, and angry silences. Me and Gabby"—I catch the frown on Mom's face—"*Gabby and I* are trying to figure out what's happening. If there's no baby, then is one of you sick?"

"No!" Mom cries. "We're fine, just fine. Please don't worry."

Which means I'd better start worrying.

"Sometimes adults discuss things in private," she goes on. "Don't you have private conversations with your friends that you don't want Dad and me listening to?"

My burger splats down onto my coleslaw. All of a sudden everything tastes like tree bark. "So, what is it that Dad did?"

"What do you mean?" he asks sharply.

"We weren't exactly spying," Gabby begins, "but we heard you say, 'Jake Lewin, how *could* you?' What did you do, Dad, that got you busted?"

Dad stammers, "I, uh, bought a set of golf clubs."

"Yes," Mom adds quickly, "when there's a perfectly good set in the garage that was his father's."

From across the table, Gabby mouths and gives me a look that says, *Ever seen Dad play golf?*

Eye messages are crossing and colliding like cars on the road, but on a field of kitchen air: Dad and Mom from east to west, Gabby and me from north to south. All four of us come to the same intersection and decide to park it for now. But this isn't over.

7

Worry, worry, worry. That's my specialty. I worry about my parents fighting, and the pressure to salvage our robotics project, and whether we Oilers are going to win another serious league game anytime this century, and how far behind I am in learning to chant my bar mitzvah portion. It's about spies, which is about as much as I can tell you right now, even though Rabbi Kefler's been grilling me mercilessly on it for weeks.

Meanwhile, I'm back to the grind at Silver Brook. Monday's argument between Maurie Glosser and Herman Stark is over who's rich and who's not.

Herman says, "Carmina DiAngelo—poor as a peasant. She puts a quarter in the pot for staff gifts."

"She put a ten-spot in once. Saw it with my own eyes."

"Get your eyes checked. It was a buck, not a ten. Now, Ethylene Callahan, she's loaded. She used to be a big-shot exec at Oscar Mayer."

"No, it was Nathan's Famous Hot Dogs," Herman insists, and Maurie pokes me in the chest.

"Eddie, you settle it. Was it Oscar or Nathan?"

"With enough mustard, it doesn't make a difference." I hurry them along to dinner, which is, like, two hours after lunch.

It's Flambé's favorite time of the day because while everyone's in the dining room, he makes his evening rounds in search of snacks. Mrs. Callahan usually leaves him a turkey-jerky stick. (You'd think she'd leave him a hot dog.) Earl Archer keeps a water bowl outside his door to wash the jerky down.

But Mrs. Boniface hardly ever goes to the dining room, so someone on staff brings her dinner up to her apartment. The door's open now, and she's sitting at her two-seater round table, holding a fork in her fist like she's planning to stab somebody, and staring sadly at soft gray meat, mushy gray green beans, and putrid Jell-O the color of diluted blood. A teddy bear lies facedown, one ear soaking up melting Jell-O.

"Hi. Mind if I call you by your first name, Thelma?"

She nods slowly as I lift the bear out of the Jell-O. "What's your teddy's name?"

She raises one eyebrow, which tells me something, but who knows what?

Ms. Brubaker clickety-clacks down the hall and chirps, "How are we doing this evening, Thelma?" Big violation of the handbook, but hey, she's the one in charge around here. "And hello, Eddie—so glad to see you're getting friendly with our seniors."

Can she really be that cheerful 24/7? Nah. I picture her stomping around her office, flinging darts at pictures of the residents. *Take that, Mrs. Callahan! Right between the eyes, Maurie Glosser! And as for you, Halina Kempinski, bull's-eye!*

Ms. Brubaker whispers to me, "We gave Thelma the cuddly teddy to help her out of her blue mood."

Blue mood? This is dungeon-black, down-in-the-dumpster misery.

"But you don't seem to care for the stuffy, do you, Thelma?" Ms. Brubaker snatches it up and wipes the Jell-O off with a paper towel from the wall dispenser, then seems to give up on it and slam-dunks the whole mess in the trash can. "What are we going to do with you?"

The old lady turns her eyes to me. For rescue?

"Well, she likes you, Eddie. It must be your sweet nature." Which she says like *sweet nature* is one of Passover's ten plagues. She pivots toward the door.

I scoop the bear out of the trash and plop down on the chair across from Thelma. It's weird to sit here without talking, but I think it's what she needs. The bristly, soggy-eared teddy bear is as stiff as a broom. A slash of a red mouth and two black button eyes stare up at me. No movement, no sound, not even a squish. No wonder it doesn't cheer up Mrs. Boniface. She needs something with more zip.

I know just the thing.

8

Ms. Perini pulls the rattling robot out of the closet and flips his On/Off switch. Bunko churns and whimpers as he warms up, then waddles across the room, bumping into desks and walls, until he finds his destiny. He overturns the basket of Legos, sending them flying. Azmara scrambles on the floor picking up handfuls to save Bunko from embarrassment.

"You are enabling his failure," Ms. Perini says.

"Face it," I say, "Bunko's not working."

Joe agrees, and even Ms. Perini doesn't contradict me. Only Azmara believes Bunko has a brilliant future in the cosmos.

"But I have an idea," I continue. "We dismantle Bunko."

"What are you saying?!" Azmara shrieks, as if I'm threatening to suffocate her cat.

"Dismantle him and start over. We keep his sounds but tweak them for a different purpose. I'll demonstrate."

Me: "How are you today?"

Bunko: Two flat sounds, accent on the first, to mimic *okay*.

Me: "Can I talk to you?"

Bunko: A high squeal that sounds like *sure!*

Me: "I'm having a real bad day."

Bunko: His best vocalization, the whimpery sound that could mean *Sorry to hear it* or *Would you like to tell me about it?* or *I'm more pitiful than a giraffe with a sore throat*.

"Not bad," Joe says, patting Bunko on the head.

Azmara stops plinking Legos into the bucket. "A verbally interactive robot?"

"Why not? He could provide the service that people need most: listening."

"I guess we wouldn't need to worry about his coordination so much then," says Joe, thinking it through. "We could just focus on getting him to respond to human voices, with a few stock replies programmed into him."

I stomp around, high on geek power. "Let's not stop at voice recognition software or settle for guttural sounds. Words! Emotional responses!"

Azmara's getting into it too. "Let's build in face recognition. You realize what we've got here? Bunko could be a full-blown social robot!"

"Whoa, kiddos," says Ms. Perini. "Too ambitious. You're talking big time, big bucks. Frankly, y'all are not ready for such a complex project yet."

Azmara sinks into a chair, a deflated tire. "Okaaay. But this is only the beginning, team. Dream big. Imagine what we can do when we're in high school."

"Meanwhile," Ms. Perini says, "I think the simplest form of this idea is achievable. We'll requisition some different materials. I'll get the principal to fork over a few bucks for a new, improved Bunko to take to regionals."

My imagination soars. "Bunko's not the right name for a verbally interactive robot. Anybody got a better idea?" I have a name in mind, but we might as well make this a team effort.

"Homunculus?" suggests Joe.

"Accurate, but not very user friendly," Azmara says.

They run through some more options: Woofie . . . Shocker . . . Rhombus . . . Wimpy . . .

"How about Zippy?" I stare up at the ceiling as if the name dropped out of the acoustic tiles.

"Zippy. Hmm, has possibilities," Joe concedes.

"All right, Zippy's the working name," says Ms. Perini, who's probably lost patience with this tangent. "And we've got our work cut out for us. We might have to add another morning."

We all shout at once: "NO!" Even Zippy.

9

When I get to Silver Brook, I'm still distracted with my grand plans for Zippy until Maurie corners me in the lobby. "Hey, Harry, Joey, Eddie, whatever—you haven't seen my diamond tie pin by any chance, have you? I wore it just the other day for Walter's celebration of life thingie, but I've torn my place apart and there's no sign of it."

I offer to help him search for it. After a sweep of the common areas turns up nothing, I start knocking on residents' apartment doors to ask if they've seen the missing pin. When I get to Earl Archer's apartment, he yells from inside, "Door's unlocked. Come in, quick!"

He's got one knobby leg stuck straight out his window. For security, the windows in the building only open about twelve inches, so here he is, bent in half, chin poking his chest, and the window smashing his back. One suspender is caught on the ledge and stretched like a bungee cord.

"What are you doing, Mr. Archer?"

"Escaping! What does it look like?"

"Why out the window?"

"Trying to do it without her catching me."

"*Her* who, Mr. Archer?"

"Rebecca Perlmuter! Who else? I'm going to the jewelry story on Fairbanks. Don't just stand there, sonny, help me. I'm folded."

What should I do? Try to stuff him back in, or help him escape? "Tell me why you're going to the jewelry store, and maybe I can help you get there."

"To buy Rebecca a big fat diamond engagement ring. I figure once I've sunk a significant wad of greenbacks into a ring, she can't turn me down."

"Um, I'm pretty sure that's not how it works, Mr. Archer . . ."

"You'll see, sonny. Someday you'll be head over heels for a gorgeous woman like I am."

She's ninety years old! "Sorry, but—"

"You can say that again. My sorry butt's stuck. Can't get the left leg in or the right one out. See? My trick knee locked. All that yoga to limber me up, and I'm *still* stuck like a barnacle."

"Wait here."

"I got any choice?"

"I'll get Clara. She'll know what to do."

"Smart idea, sonny. Make it quick, but don't let Rebecca find out about this. If she sees me bent like a palm tree in a hurricane, she'll lose respect for me and won't marry me to live out our best years together."

I rush up to the fitness center. Mrs. Dorian is clutching the banisters and slowly walking up and down three steps that go nowhere. I remember something like that in preschool. With his one good arm, Maurie Glosser aims something that looks like a short fishing rod with a sock dangling from it, and he's trying to wiggle his foot into the sock. In another corner, Mrs. Callahan is knitting a pukey-green scarf long enough to stretch down I-35 from Oklahoma City to Dallas.

Clara, the OT, glides from one to the other, giving them pointers.

"Clara, quick! Mr. Archer is stuck in his window!"

She signals her assistant to cover for her, and we

sprint down the hall. "He should've used his medical alert button," Clara says breathlessly as Hank joins us on the way to the elevator. Oh, right—the handbook mentioned those buttons. People wear them like watches on their wrists or on lanyards around their necks.

"Oh, mercy me," Clara declares with a laugh when she sees Mr. Archer folded like an omelet. "How did you manage that shenanigan, sweet man?" She gently instructs him on how to unlock his knee. With me holding up the window and Hank dragging poor Mr. Archer by his armpits, we get him unstuck a split second before the window comes slicing down like a guillotine.

Once he's stretched out in his lounge chair, rubbing his trick knee, Mr. Archer says, "By Jove, I almost made it. Next time I will. You, sonny, are my hero. You're a regular Superman."

And people say nothing ever happens in a seniors' home? Ha! A ghost, a thief, an escape artist, a hot romance, and how could you even *try* to describe Lina Kempinski?

10

As usual, Tessa and I are the last ones to get picked up after b'nai mitzvah class. The cold drizzle plasters my hair to my forehead like an ancient Roman helmet.

Tessa tames her wet hair enough to wrap it into a top knot, which looks so tight that I half expect it to shout *ouch!* She's cute in the same way that a chipmunk with nuts in his cheeks is cute.

"What's going on at Silver Brook?" she asks.

"Toibe the Ghost is up to her tricks, according to Lina. And some residents are complaining about things missing from their apartments. Coincidence?"

Tessa snorts. "They don't remember where they put their teeth, never mind their treasures."

"Yeah, but even the ones with working memories are missing stuff."

"What kind of stuff? The week I was there, Mr. Stark lost one shoe of a pair, Mrs. Dorian lost a hairbrush, and Mr. Archer lost a tin Altoids box full of paper clips. Nothing that's gonna sell on the black market."

"Well, someone took Mrs. Callahan's husband's gold watch and Mr. Glosser's diamond tie pin."

"So, lemme get this straight," Tessa says, unwinding a rope of curls until it hits her shoulder. "You're saying the ghost of Lina's twin doesn't just stop clocks and talk to her through the heating vent and freeze her out, but Toibe actually creeps into *other* people's apartments to pilfer stuff?"

"You said it, I didn't. I'm just telling you the word that's on the street. Here comes my mom."

"Why am I always the last one to get picked up? Seven hundred and eighty more days, and I can drive myself anywhere I want." Tessa peers at my car as it glides toward us. "Looks like your dad again, unless your mom suddenly went bald."

I sling my backpack over one shoulder. "Come back to Silver Brook and check out the ghostly thief yourself. You must have at least twenty hours left of your mitzvah project. Why not finish them up where you started them? At least you'll have company now."

"So . . . you're begging me to come back?"

"No! Well, kind of."

"I love it. Beg a little more?"

"Forget it.'"

She grins. "Okay, I'm in. But I'm not going back because you asked me to."

"Sure. It's because you love the oldies."

"Shame, shame, Lewin. The politically correct designation is *seniors*," Tessa informs me. "Old seniors, not the kind applying to college. And honestly, I do miss some of them. Lina Kempinski, not so much. But Maurie and Herman—and that sweet old couple, the Goldfarbs. It's so adorable the way she's the ventriloquist for him, while he's way out in left field."

"On a different field, different ballpark."

"Different planet." Tessa channels Ruth Goldfarb: "'Oh, I understand, Sidney, my dumpling, you'd like to strip down to your *Spider-Man* skivvies and wrestle a fourteen-foot alligator, but we don't have many here in Oklahoma, so keep your sweatpants on, my darling. Would you settle for a strawberry nutrition shake instead?' What do you think, Lewin? Did I hit it?"

"On the button." I let the reference to my

Spider-Man boxers go by without comment. I guess word of my disastrous slide during the last Oilers game has gotten around. "So, Mondays or Wednesdays, four to five?"

"Wednesdays. Mondays I have taekwondo."

"Maybe you could teach some kicks to the Goldfarbs."

"It's a deal."

You have to respect a girl with her talents, especially since she could probably break me in half with one well-aimed kick.

11

Zippy stands like a department store mannequin with his dome head and his empty eye holes and a curvy thing that's supposed to look like a smiling mouth, except that we didn't get the up-curves just right, so he looks more like a demented Chucky doll. His feet—well, two wheels and a caster for stability—are covered by a fire-engine-red strip, and the rest of him is painted white, except for a red sign over his belly that announces to the world, *HI! I'M YOUR FRIEND ZIPPY!!!*

"Lose the exclamation points," advises Azmara. "Makes him seem too fake."

"He *is* fake." Joe opens Zippy's back door with a push of two fingers to expose impressive guts, including his On/Off toggle switch.

Ms. Perini circles Zippy. "He could use a fedora

so he doesn't look so much like a techno-snowman."

"No!" Azmara shouts, slapping both hands on Zippy's head. "Wow, he hums, even turned off."

Joe says, "Because he likes you. He wants to go to the Spring Stomp with you."

"Awesome, although he's kind of short for me. But then, so are you guys."

Time to unveil the rest of my plan. "Hey, what if Zippy's not a boy?"

"A man?" Joe asks, totally confused.

Azmara's eyes widen. "I get it, Eddie. You think Zippy's a girl!"

"Aw, come on," says Joe. "Could he be nonbinary? Girl robots are dumb."

"Not true!" I tell him. "Why should a girl robot be any less interesting or cool than a girl human? Zippy can be a super-impressive girl android. Like Velma Staplebot from *The Lego Movie*."

Still skeptical, Joe steps back to size Zippy up. "A girl, really? We'd have to give her some earrings or lipstick."

"A hijab?" Azmara jokes, tugging at the pin on hers.

"Zippy doesn't need clothes or jewelry or makeup," I say. "But I think we could adjust her face a little. If she's going to be interactive, she should have a friendly face, right? The kind of face a lonely person would feel comfortable talking to."

"Maybe . . . eyelashes?" Joe tries.

"Never mind eyelashes." Azmara's breathless with excitement. "Bigger, rounder, kinder eyes."

Ideas start pulsing out. "Eyes with pupils."

"Softer eyes, not that searchlight blue."

"And open-close eyelids."

"Her mouth could be rounder, maybe more O-shaped, like she's surprised or sympathetic."

Joe mutters, "You want her to look like the Pillsbury Doughboy girl?"

I turn to the boss. "What do you think, Ms. Perini?"

"Build it. Go for it, but don't forget the guts inside."

"Right," I say. "Let's see how her VEX Cortex microcontroller brain works." I tap computer keys, and Joe flips Zippy's power switch with a dramatic flair like an orchestra conductor. Her blue lights flash through the empty eye holes. So far, so good!

"Move him, uh, her," Joe orders, and I hit the command keys. We have Zippy working in a C program in VEX DR, and she glides like a puppy skidding across a tile floor, then corrects herself when she gets too close to a chair or a wall. Great! No more Legos.

Azmara claps her hands. "She's way more intelligent than Bunko ever was."

Ms. Perini frowns. "She still wobbles. That won't go over well at regionals."

Zippy is turned off and set on her side so we can adjust the wheels.

"Left one's a little loose." Joe wrenches the wheel and caster tighter, and Zippy's back on her feet, blue light shining. We've gotta do something about the wild fire-engine-red trim. But at least we've made a start.

12

Tessa's back at Silver Brook this afternoon. We meet up out front, where Hank is helping Mrs. Callahan into the Silver Brook van to go to her weekly meeting with her psychic.

"Check out that fruit-basket hat!" murmurs Tessa. The gravity of plastic fruit drags the rim down over Mrs. Callahan's eyes but doesn't stop her from spotting us. She waves, and Tessa waves back. "She's so cool. The week I was here, she told me that back in the 1960s she marched on the state capitol to end segregation in restaurants and movie theaters. She got arrested with a bunch of other protesters. Can you imagine that? Mrs. Callahan in jail!"

I bet that's where she'd like to send the thief who stole her watch.

We head up to the front door, and Tessa spots

Lina through the glass. "Think she's changed those socks since I was here last?"

"Don't try to peel them off. They're epoxied to her feet."

"Hey, Lewin, let's promise we're never getting old, okay?"

"You want to die young?"

"No! I want to *stay* young until I'm ninety. Then I'll quit bungee jumping and age gracefully." She sticks out her hand for me to shake. "Agreed?"

Together till we're ninety? I can live with that. If it works for geese, why not for us? "Agreed."

Inside, Lina greets Tessa in her warm, fuzzy way: "Who invited *you*?"

"Nice to see you too."

We're inspected like we're Lina's 4-H blue-ribbon hogs. "You're a mess, Eddie Whatever. When's the last time those denims saw the inside of a washer?"

Tessa flares. "You're in no position to talk. Those horrid red socks could walk on their own."

Lina turns to me. "She a friend of yours?"

"The best." And dang if I'm not blushing. Again. The curse of a pale, freckled face. But I don't think Tessa notices because Flambé comes barreling down the hall.

"Flamboozle, baby!" The dog, who still isn't speaking to me, is all over Tessa.

While they're rolling around on the floor, I'm shifting from foot to foot so I don't step on them.

Lina growls, "Stand still, you're making me dizzy." She's fiddling with a fidget spinner, but her crooked fingers can't get the hang of it, so she tosses it to me before she swings around to glare at Tessa. "You didn't ask, but I'll tell you anyway. Toibe's still here to make my life miserable. Whenever she's not haunting my apartment, I hear her bumbling around in the basement under my bedroom."

Tessa pushes *Flamboozle* off her. The dog scrambles to his feet, snarls at me, and retreats in a snit. When the fidget spinner whizzing between my thumb and middle finger captures Lina's attention, I ask, "Do you actually *see* her, Lina? See a ghost up close and personal?"

"Certainly. Me, I'm about the size of a fat Thanksgiving turkey, but Toibe's bigger."

"You mean in your imagination?" Tessa asks.

"No, in my memory."

Which reminds me of Mrs. DiAngelo: *That ghost steals our memories.*

"I don't get the turkey thing."

"That's your problem, boychik, not mine."

Man, talking to Lina is like hanging by your feet from monkey bars. Everything's upside down. I toss her back the spinner, which she studies as if she's looking for the On/Off switch.

Thunk, thunk: the Goldfarbs inch their way out of the dayroom toward us, hunched over their walkers.

"Look, Sidney, it's our favorite bat mitzvah girl, Tessa! We've missed you, dear. You look swell-elegant today. My husband's words, not mine."

"Hi, Mrs. Goldfarb. I wish I had a grandmother like you. My one grandma is still a 1960s hippie, and the other one raises Vietnamese potbellied pigs. Neither one is a cookie-baking bubbie."

Mrs. Goldfarb steadies herself with one hand and wraps the other around Tessa. "I'll see if the kitchen folks will let me turn out a few dozen Toll House cookies. No, Sidney, no walnuts. I know those crumbs get under your dentures. Well, excuse us, Tessa, dear. We need to spruce up for dinner."

I have to agree. Her wig's on crooked, or else one ear has moved south.

Tessa and I regroup over by the reception desk, where Judy's distracted by the security guard, Officer Kinsey, as usual.

"So," I say quietly to Tessa, "if there was a ghost here at Silver Brook, and I'm not saying there is, what's the best place to hunt for her?"

"*Her?*"

"According to Lina."

"Hmm." Tessa speculates: "Maybe it's not a ghost but some evil creature hunkering in the shadows, just to freak everyone out."

"Yeah, and it's hiding the stolen goods in the janitor's closet or the attic."

"Or," Tessa gasps, "the basement!"

13

Tessa leads me through the kitchen and down a set of steep, narrow stairs, slowing down on the last step. The basement is all dark corners, menacing under-table tunnels, flickery shadows. A window almost as high as the ceiling is covered with decaying leaves and lets in about two watts of light. The chilly, damp air smells like rotten rodent flesh—confirmed when we spot a squirrel behind a ripped cane chair, its bushy tail standing up stiff.

"Ugggggh." Tessa pulls her shirt collar up over her nose. "Must have dropped dead for lack of food and water."

"Hey, I've got it! It's the ghost of the squirrel that's haunting Silver Brook. Toibe the Squirrel."

"Get real, Lewin. What's *that*?" Tessa points to a gizmo sticking out of a carton.

"Something out of a medieval torture chamber. A grunchet-grabber-twister."

"Could be." She lifts heavy gray steel a couple of inches. "Oh, I know! It's an old-fashioned meat grinder. My hippie grandma had one before she got her Cuisinart. A nasty ghost has lots of uses for a meat grinder."

I squeeze between sealed cartons and drums of paint and turpentine and flick through a pile of paintbrushes with their bristles glopped together as stiff as the squirrel's tail. "Wish we had a flashlight."

What if the basement door slams shut, and we get stuck down here forever? We'd end up as dead and stiff as the squirrel. In fact, the squirrel would be our last meal. Eww, all that hair in my mouth.

What if there really is a ghost, and it slides through a wall and wraps its cloudy arms around Tessa and she dies of shock? Which would be better than eating that hairy squirrel. What if Tessa's potbellied-pig-raising grandma blames me for luring Tessa back to Silver Brook and decides to extract vengeance?

Tessa puts a sudden stop to my wild thoughts by pulling her phone out of her jeans pocket. Clunk my forehead: Why didn't I think of that?

Playing the light around the cinder block walls

and cement floor, she shudders and backs toward the stairs. Her voice shakes as she says, "Come on, before Madame Brubaker notices us missing."

Tessa and I almost spontaneously combust on our way up the narrow basement stairs. In the safety of the kitchen, she says, "Let's review what we learned down there on our brave quest for the ghost-thief of Silver Brook."

I make two thumb–and–index-finger zeroes.

"Exactly."

"So what now?"

"Well," Tessa says, "Lina did say she heard someone moving around down there. She may not be a reliable source, but the easiest way to find out if anything sinister's going on would be to set up a camera."

"Good point!" I say. "Maybe we should talk to Hank about that."

"Or maybe we do it ourselves. I can use my family's old baby cam that we got when my brother was born. Every time he snorted or pooped my parents ran into his room."

"Nah, a baby cam's too limited," I protest.

"Oh, you're thinking we need a high-tech surveillance camera, like for superspies." Tessa taps away at her phone. "Wireless or wired? One camera or eight? Here's one no bigger than a lipstick. Oh, this one looks like a hair dryer. It's got three-sixty capability. Wait, no night vision."

"Yeah, gotta have night vision because it's eternally midnight down there where squirrels go to die." While Tessa's becoming the world's greatest expert on spy cameras, I'm hatching one of my brilliant ideas.

She turns the phone toward me. "Hey, look, you can get a total security system starting at a mere seven hundred dollars. You got that in your piggy bank? I'm voting for the baby cam."

I shake my head. "Overruled. Listen, I can *build* a spy camera that'll outperform your little baby cam."

"You can do that? I mean, A, is it legal? And B, are you a genius?"

"Legal? Who knows. But genius, absolutely. If I can build an interactive robot, how hard can a spy camera be?"

Turns out, it's harder than you'd think without Azmara's help. She's the High Nerd on our robotics squad. I'm a hack compared to her. Or, if I'm being kind to myself, let's say a minor genius. So I've been working on the wireless spy cam from a kit. Gabby's offered to help me in exchange for two weeks of my allowance, so she barks the instructions to me, reminding me how clueless and clumsy I am.

We've been at this for an hour. My game starts in thirty minutes, and Joe is already in our driveway, beeping his bike horn.

Gabby grabs the canister out of my hand. "Leave this to the expert. It's child's play." She forgets that she's a child, but I'm okay handing it over because I'd rather not electrocute myself before our game.

14

Oilers against the Sooners, tied 3–3, top of the ninth, two outs, Sooners up. Coach calls a time-out.

Joe says, "Think Coach will put me in at shortstop?"

"Sheesh, if you don't know, who would? He's your dad."

"Yeah, but tricky times like this, he likes to keep Otis at short."

"Erdman!" Coach shouts. He calls his son by their last name so it doesn't look like he plays favorites. "Sprint out there to shortstop. You, Otis, take the bench."

Kicking dirt, Otis grumbles, "Aw, Coach, I was just getting warmed up." But Coach points his no-nonsense finger at the bench.

So we Oilers trot out there in our best-chance

positions: me at first, Joe at short, Wallace and Jackson at second and third, and a couple of good guys deep in the outfield. Ranson warms up on the mound. You can smell the burst of hope. Other teams have been calling us Soilers instead of Oilers, but here's our chance to show them who has the grease to break our eight-game losing streak. With the game tied, all we need is to hold the Sooners, then score one little run to win. One little run.

Uh-oh. Their biggest hitter, a twelve-year-old who probably shaves twice a day, screws up his eyes to spook our pitcher. Ranson fires one right over the plate for a slick strike. Second pitch, not so lucky. The big guy's bat makes solid contact, and he smashes a long fly toward the fence.

But before the guy touches first, our second baseman, Wallace, spears the ball and slings it toward me. Never thought my leg could stretch that far. Is it the flamingo practice?

The guy falls like a sack of potatoes. The ump calls, "Out!" Suddenly the inning's over, and it's all on our shoulders.

"Lewin, you're up," Coach yells.

My shoulders.

When I step up to the plate for the first pitch,

I hear Gabby's voice bellowing over the crowd, "Knock 'em dead, sweetcakes!" Nothing embarrassing about my sister.

But I. Am. On. Fire. I taste triumph and the victory pizza Coach promised. I run through my ritual: two practice swings, cap adjustment, knock on the helmet, snap my wristband, tap dirt from my cleats with my bat and—here comes the pitch!

I let two called strikes go by. Too much pressure. The next pitch, I just about kill that curveball. *Crack!* The ball streaks into the field, then careens into the outfield, past the desperate lunge of the Sooners' third baseman. Dang if it isn't my first home run. I sprint to home plate with my scrawny arms raised in victory, and—first time ever—I'm mobbed by the rest of the Oilers.

"That's the game," yells the ump, and we all file through the Sooners, high-fiving and good-gaming, until Coach Erdman shouts, "Peeeeetzaaaah!"

It's a winning streak, one in a row.

<hr/>

After the pizza, I bike home with Joe. He's a half mile ahead of me on the Burlington bike path. A city bus wheedles in between our bikes while Joe churns away on the pedals as if he's got a meeting with a major league scout in two minutes. When the bus pulls out, I shout to Joe's muddy backside, "Wait up."

He slows down and jams his foot to the street to stop his bike until I catch up. Now we're coasting side by side, kind of like the Goldfarbs with their walkers.

"Hey, Joe, I've got a question. So, if your parents keep huddling behind closed doors and whispering things they don't want you to hear, and they can't look each other in the eye, and your dad turns into a grump overnight, and your mom is a basket case . . . I'm just saying . . . what would you think was going on?"

"Simple," Joe says. "I'd think they were getting a divorce. Mine did."

Suddenly my stomach drops to my knees. I speed up and pass Joe. I can't look him in the face, so my butt might as well be what's in his line of vision.

Before I'm even in the living room, I blubber the divorce theory to Gabby.

"No! I won't allow it!" she hollers.

"We have to stop this, and we have to do it now."

"You do the talking."

We tromp into the family room, where Mom and Dad are sitting on separate chairs, not cuddling on the couch like they used to. Dad's actually watching *Jeopardy.* Daytime. Unheard of in the Lewin house!

I glance at the screen, thinking, *Divorce for five hundred,* and suck in my breath to launch the first missile. "Mom, Dad, remember the other night when we were talking about things being out of whack around here?"

Mom tosses down a *Time* magazine. "No, we're not having a baby."

Gabby shoots me the go-ahead sign with her jaw clenched tight.

"So, we've figured out what's going on." Gulp.

Before I can get any further, Gabby cries, "We're getting a divorce, aren't we?"

Dad bounds off his chair and rushes over to Mom, motioning for Gabby and me to join him. "No, kids, we are not getting a divorce. It's . . . it's . . ."

Mom kisses Gabby's head—mine too—and clutches Dad's hand. "It's time we drew you into what's going on. Your dad lost his job."

"*Quit* my job. I was miserable, overworked, and underpaid. My boss was a tyrant, and I couldn't take it a day longer, so I quit. Against your mother's better judgment."

Mom licks her lips and sighs. "The timing . . . bills," she says vaguely.

Dad zaps off the TV. "We didn't want to worry you two while this was brewing. We've discussed how to manage temporarily without my salary."

"Are we going to lose the house?" Gabby asks. "Are we going to have to *downsize*?"

Dad laughs a little. "Don't worry, kids. I'll find another store that needs a good, experienced produce manager. A guy who really knows his veggies. Till then, we've got savings. We'll be fine, just fine."

Mom flashes fake cheer. "We have so much to look forward to—Eddie's bar mitzvah in June and Gabby's tenth birthday in July. My baby, a whole decade old!"

Pulling Gabby and me into his arms, Dad says, "And you've got that robotics competition coming up, right? Lots of positive stuff going on."

It all sounds upbeat and encouraging, except for the sadness in Dad's voice and the worried look on Mom's face. If I'm a champion worrier, she's world class.

I can't wait to get back to Silver Brook, where things are simpler than at home.

15

First thing Monday afternoon, I sneak down to the basement and set up the spy camera that Gabby and I—well, essentially just Gabby—put together. There's no way it can get a full view of the room, but I plant it in a spot where it'll catch anyone coming down the stairs. When that's done, I get back to my regularly scheduled senior time.

I can tell Mrs. Boniface wants company because she's sitting in her doorway again. She's wearing that scarf I saw Mrs. Callahan knitting, even though the temperature in this building is tropical. One half of her face sags more than before. I heard she had another small stroke. They're as common as hiccups around here.

When I stop to say hi, she backs up her wheelchair and gives me room to step inside her apartment.

I settle in for a conversation. By *conversation* I mean, I talk and she floats up in the ozone. She drifts back down to Planet Earth when I say, "You've probably heard about the thief. You're not missing anything, are you?"

She raises her hand and rubs the pale indentation where a ring used to be.

"Your ring's gone?"

Slow nod.

"Sheesh, the one Mr. Boniface gave you?" He passed away years ago. No kids, which is why it's a mystery who's sending rent checks to Silver Brook every month.

"Man, I'm so sorry, Thelma. Do you have any idea who could've taken it?"

Head shake in slo-mo.

It has to be somebody who's reasonably mobile and nimble. I mentally scroll through the possible suspects.

- Hank, the maintenance guy? No, if anybody is on the up-and-up, it's Hank. Although he does have a lot of mouths to feed. A few extra bucks could be tempting.

- Mrs. Callahan? Her closet is jammed with fancy dresses and round drums of hats with ribbons and feathers and fruit and other stuff right out of Mother Nature's hat factory. How does she pay for all that and her weekly visits to the psychic? Hmm. On the other hand, she had a watch stolen. Doesn't that get her off the hook?

- Either Maurie or Herman? Maurie with his double walking sticks tap-tapping down the hall like an over-the-hill cross-country skier? Herman arguing with Maurie about whose room to invade and when? More likely both of them. One wouldn't trust the other to do it alone. But no, the Silver Brook burglar has to be sneakier and a lot quieter than those two.

- Mrs. DiAngelo? She's convinced the thief is a ghost who stole her memories. Whole hours go by that she doesn't remember later. Could they have been spent raiding her neighbors' apartments while everybody was at lunch?

- A staff member with key-card access to the apartments? I can't imagine Clara or Lupita as criminal masterminds. I'm pretty sure Judy doesn't have key cards, and anyway she's always busy at the front desk. And who's always hanging over her desk . . . ?

- Officer Kinsey! Could he be the thief? Nah, that makes no sense. What kind of a security guy wants a bunch of robberies going on at his place? He'd have to risk losing his job, or at least his reputation.

And now here comes Ms. Brubaker to ruin our whole non-conversation.

"How *are* we this afternoon, Thelma? I hope you're enjoying Eddie's delightful company! I suppose you know, Eddie, that Mrs. Boniface has lost her wedding ring." She has a way of talking in front of the residents as though they're not there, but Mrs. Boniface's eyes say she's heard every word.

As if she just figured out that the silent lady is still breathing, Ms. Brubaker says, "It'll turn up, hon, don't worry." She pats Mrs. Boniface's hand the way you'd pat a little kid's head.

When Ms. Brubaker leaves, I say, "Guess what, Thelma. My robotics squad is working on something special for you."

Her thin eyebrow slides up, which says a lot, for her.

16

The tree hovering over Silver Brook's back patio—
elm? maple? all trees look alike to me—anyway, this
one gives up a dead leaf that zeroes in on Mr. Goldfarb. He doesn't even blink when Mrs. Goldfarb bats
it away. Just keeps staring out at the pond. What if he's
already dead? What if Mrs. Goldfarb stuffed him and
glued his hands to his walker? A squirrel up in the tree
stares down at us with beady black-dot eyes. He probably thinks I killed his buddy in the basement.

All these flowers around, and I'm sneezing like a
fiend when Lina rolls out to the patio.

Mrs. Goldfarb says, "Why look, Sidney, it's our
next-door neighbor."

Mr. Goldfarb clumps his walker a few steps away.
Guess he's still alive.

Lina sneers at the Goldfarbs, until she gets

distracted by my sneezing. "What's the matter with you, Eddie Whatever?"

"Allergy."

She hands me a soggy tissue from inside her sleeve.

"Uh, thanks. How's your day going, Lina?" Whoops. I forgot the wisdom of the volunteer handbook: never ask a resident a question if you don't want to listen to the answer for the next hour.

"She wouldn't give me a moment's peace last night."

"Who?" I ask, stuffing the tissue into my pocket until I can find a trash can.

"Who do you think? Toibe!"

"Oh, yeah, your ghost-sister who's not much bigger than a hefty turkey." It's so ridiculous that I have to bite my tongue and flare my nostrils to get under control. A snort escapes anyway. "What does Toibe's voice sound like?"

"Don't you listen? I already told you Toibe doesn't talk in her own voice. She uses a man's voice, to scare me."

"I don't get it, Lina. Why would your sister—"

"Twin sister."

"Yeah, why would she speak to you through the heating vent in a man's voice?"

"To torment me. She's relentless."

Also nonexistent. Still, a dot-sized piece of doubt wedges in my brain, like a popcorn shell stuck between your teeth, and I wonder if there *is* something not quite human lurking down in the basement that freaked Tessa and me out.

If there is, I'm hoping the spy cam footage will reveal it.

"Come along, my darling Sidney," Mrs. Goldfarb commands. "There's a show in the dayroom before dinner. Let's get good seats." Puppy-dog Sidney follows her inside.

"Will you be okay out here alone, Lina?" I ask. "Because Mrs. DiAngelo asked me to clear some junk off her dresser before her kids from Lawton come."

"She smuggled them out one by one."

"The stuff from Mrs. DiAngelo's dresser?"

Lina looks at me sharply. "Why are you staring at me?"

"Because you said something strange, Lina." Again.

"Didn't say a word."

"Yeahhhh, okay." In the weeks I've been coming to Silver Brook, the lady has turned weirder and weirder. And those red socks? They're starting to ferment.

"One by one, in a toolbox."

"Okay, sure, a toolbox. Do you want to expand on that?"

"I must never, ever tell anyone."

Which doesn't give me much to work with. "Okay. Great talking to you, Lina." I edge past the nosy squirrel, into the building.

On Tuesday afternoon, I'm the first one in the synagogue conference room until Rabbi Kefler rushes in, hot and sweaty, with a towel draped around his neck. "Glad the others aren't here yet, Eliahu. Gives me time to cool off. I've been shooting baskets with the confirmation class." He takes a deep breath and smears sweat across his face. "Whew, better." He grins. Those dimples—does he store marbles in them while he sleeps? "How's your mitzvah project going?"

"It's been . . . pretty weird, Rabbi. Lina Kempinski. I think she's getting loonier."

"Is that a professional psychiatric diagnosis, Dr. Lewin?"

"Not exactly, but you know she talks that ghost

stuff about her twin sister. She swears the twin is talking to her through the heating vent, but in a man's voice."

Rabbi Kefler looks troubled. He lets the towel slide to the floor. "So what makes you think she's getting—how did you put it?—loonier?"

"Okay, this: yesterday, out of nowhere, Lina said, *She smuggled them out one by one.* Made no sense, and when I asked her about it, she insisted she hadn't said a word. That's gotta qualify as loony."

I can't decode the strange look on the rabbi's face. "Lina has some memory problems."

"You mean she's losing it?" The thief is stealing her memories, same as Mrs. DiAngelo?

"I mean she remembers things that are too hard to bring into her conscious life. Things she's not pre-pared to share with others. And also, yes, she's los-ing it, as you put it so delicately." The other b'nai mitzvah kids are messing around out in the hall, so the rabbi quickly says, "We'll talk some more about this another time, Eddie. Oops, I called you by your American name. Don't tell the others. They'd tease me mercilessly."

Hey, wait till everybody else hears!

17

In Ms. Perini's lab, Azmara enters strings of code faster than I can blink. Every so often Ms. Perini makes a correction in the trail of alpha-numeric soup that sloshes across Azmara's screen.

Meanwhile, Joe tweaks the hardware that magically turns Zippy wireless, and I work on things like softening the fire-engine-red trimmings that might knock Mrs. Boniface off her chair. Zippy's now a user-friendly sky blue.

Quickly—and by that I mean five hours of work later—we get her stumbling around by a press of a clicker. Still a long way to go. No chance for a first at regionals, but Zippy may qualify for the Humanitarian Ribbon, given to a robot that does community service. I guess some robots have mitzvah projects too.

"She's ready for the real test. Let's go for sounds," Azmara says.

My fingers fly over the keys, but Zippy's basic mutters are as much as we're going to get out of her without a ton more time and money. Anyway, four or five semi-words might be enough for Mrs. Boniface, who has none.

"She needs to respond to a human voice," I remind the squad. "Especially a female voice."

Azmara speaks into Zippy's microphone receiver: "I'M HAPPY TO SEE YOU, ZIPPY."

There's a two-second delay while no one breathes. Suddenly Zippy comes to the party in all her high-pitched whimper-y glory: "UH HEEEEK BRRR."

"We are brilliant!" I yell. But we still have a lot of work to do before we can take Zippy out into the field for a test drive with Mrs. Boniface.

"Have you checked the spy cam yet?" Tessa asks me when she shows up at Silver Brook ten minutes late.

"Yeah, but so far it's just dead air. Nobody's been down there since I set it up on Monday."

"Well, we'll keep an eye on it. What's going on in here?"

At least fifty seniors are parked in the dayroom, facing a curtain that's been rigged up in the front. "There's some kind of performance today," I explain to Tessa. Occasionally school choirs and middle-aged cover bands drop by to entertain the residents. Judging by the attendance this afternoon, this show must be a big deal. Frank Sinatra back from the dead, at least.

Corny forties tunes blast out of the loudspeakers. *"Don't sit under the apple tree with anyone else but me . . ."* Sung by some bubbly harmonizing women.

"They call this *music*?" Tessa whispers.

But I notice that Mrs. DiAngelo's bouncing in her chair. "That was our song, Antony's and mine. The purple apple tree. Oh, and remember 'Boogie Woogie Bugle Boy of Company B'?" Seniors nod and sing along. "Antony and I, we must have jitterbugged to that record a thousand times!"

I offer, "Want to dance, Mrs. DiAngelo?"

"Oh, my, no. My arthuritis . . ."

Some folks doze, some mess with fidget spinners, some knit. False teeth click in time to the music. Tessa perches next to Mrs. Goldfarb, who's tapping her old-lady black shoe to the music, but she's too busy listening to what Mr. Goldfarb doesn't say to catch the beat. Is he blinking in Morse code?

Bored, Flambé settles on his huge velvet couch cushion, snoring like he needs his tonsils out. Mrs. Perlmuter, the yoga lady, waltzes around the room, trying to drag the men up as partners.

Maurie Glosser's face burns radish-red when she sits on his lap.

"Go for it, Maurie!" jokes Herman Stark. "Might be your last chance, you old geezer."

"Aw, go soak your head!" snaps Maurie.

Mrs. Perlmuter moves on to Earl Archer, who hand-combs his Albert Einstein white hair and dances once around the room with her. "Why, if I were sixty years younger, I'd marry you, Rebecca!"

Mrs. Perlmuter sniffs. "If I were sixty years younger, I'd be hoofing it on Broadway with Fred Astaire."

Tessa says, "Look at Lina over there with her straw-yellow hair wound up in some knotty circle around her head."

"Think she's spiking a fever, her cheeks all pinked up like that?"

"It's rouge, Lewin. You brush it on your cheeks. Lina's gone all out for this."

Ms. Brubaker twists out from behind the curtain and yells into a microphone so loud that the drapes flutter. "Friends, you are in for a treat!"

"If it ain't chocolate, it's no treat," yells Maurie Glosser.

Ms. Brubaker ignores him. "Are you ready?" she shouts into the audience.

And Lina says, "Bring it on."

"As promised in our daily BrookBites, we have a world-renowned actor here to dazzle us with Shakespearean soliloquies. Let's hear it for the one and only . . ."

Ivan, I think automatically, which was my favorite book in fourth grade. But Ms. Brubaker isn't talking about a caged gorilla and his elephant buddy.

". . . Canto Caliberti!" She yanks the curtain open, and there stands an old man in snazzy gray pants with a sharp crease down each leg and a maroon dress-up jacket with a sky-blue handkerchief pointing out of the pocket like a fence picket. He raises his arms dramatically and bellows loudly enough to set Mrs. DiAngelo's hearing aids squealing:

"TO BE, OR NOT TO BE, THAT IS THE QUESTION!"

"What's he yelling about?" asks Mrs. Dorian.

"It's Shakespeare," someone answers.

Mr. Caliberti scowls at the audience, clears his throat, and starts again. "To be, or not to be, that is the question."

"I don't get it, what's the question?" Mrs. Callahan, this time, speaking around the unlit cigar clenched between her teeth.

Mrs. DiAngelo scolds the audience. "Just hush and listen, because the gentleman is heavenly with that elegant purple voice. A little old for Hamlet, but nice."

By the time the actor gets to the "slings and arrows of outrageous fortune," he's totally lost his audience, and Herman Stark is demanding popcorn.

Ms. Brubaker starts a round of applause. "Thank you so much, Mr. Caliberti! I'm afraid our guests are a little distracted right now. Everyone's fresher in the morning."

"Ah, yes," the actor says in his fake British accent, "I have faced every manner of audience worldwide in my long and illustrious career. Next time I shall bring my beloved cat to delight the audience."

"Does your cat do Shakespeare too?" asks Mrs. Dorian.

"Me, I like dogs." Mr. Archer stretches out his

striped legs and kicks up his feet. "My dogs are barkin' after that dance with Rebecca."

Ms. Brubaker says, "I have fabulous news for you, my friends. Mr. Caliberti is going to lend his inestimable talents to us at Silver Brook. He'll be teaching an informal performing arts class. How many would like to join?"

Not one raised hand, until Lina says, "Sign me up."

"Just Lina? Well, the class will be here in the dayroom on Tuesday mornings if any of the rest of you decide you're interested." She checks her watch and looks disappointed by what it tells her.

That's it? That's her pitch?

"Is there going to be music?" I blurt out.

Ms. Brubaker gives me a blank look, but Mr. Caliberti says, "I intended the class to concentrate on theater, but *musical* theater is certainly a vital element of the performing tradition. And if anyone is particularly interested in singing . . ."

Mrs. Callahan lifts her cigar holder high in the air. "I'm in!"

"Me too," says Mrs. DiAngelo happily.

I can't help grinning at Ms. Brubaker, who gives me a thin, pasted-on smile in return. Cupping her hand to her ear, she says, "I think I hear the dinner bell!"

The whole herd spins chairs and walkers and stampedes to the dining hall, but not Lina. She rolls up to Mr. Caliberti and points with her red-socked toe. "Remember me from Paris?"

Wow, I didn't see *that* coming.

18

Tessa's gone to the dining hall with the hungry mob, and I'm left with Lina and Canto Caliberti. Up close, I see that the actor has an inch of makeup spackled onto his face and little round red circles on his cheeks, level with his nostrils. All he'd need is a curly red wig and floppy shoes, and he could be Ronald McDonald.

With his glasses on the end of his nose, he squints to get a good look. "Why, Halina Kempinski, as I live and breathe. We haven't met since we sang those duets at the Rue d'Elene nightclub."

"You sang in a nightclub, Lina?" Could have blown me over!

"A cabaret. Classier than a nightclub." She wiggles her red socks. "I had gorgeous gams back then."

"You look exactly the same, Halina."

"Just fifty years older. And you're still a handsome devil. I knew you when you were Harvey Fishbein, from the Lower East Side Pickles Fishbeins."

"Long time ago, long time." Mr. Caliberti turns to me. "Pardon us, young man, as we trip the light fantastic down memory lane." There's a real twinkle in his eye. "So, Halina, you always teased me about meeting your gorgeous sister, but you never introduced us. Is she here at Silver Brook also?" He asks like it's a big joke, but Lina takes it seriously.

"You could say so." She winks at me—not the way Tessa winks, but more like when Grandpa Max slips me a ten while my parents aren't looking. Slow and serious.

"Harvey, my old friend, come with me to dinner. I'll treat you to the worst meatloaf you've ever tasted in your long and illustrious career."

After dinner, while Tessa runs downstairs to check on the spy cam and Lina goes to the nurse's station for her meds, I corner the actor who knew Lina a half century ago.

"Mr. Caliberti—or is it Mr. Fishbein?"

"You may call me Canto. That is my stage name," he says, nose up in the air. Man, he's more stuck up than Flambé.

"Yes, sir. So, I heard you ask about Lina's twin. I'm curious about her myself. Did she tell you that her sister haunts this place?"

Canto bursts into an overdone laugh, dabbing at imaginary tears. "No, my old friend failed to mention that detail." He gives me a once-over look. "You believe this?"

"Nah, I'm not into ghosts. Just curious. And a little, uh, concerned for her, I guess."

"Ah, my young chap, I have seen strange things in my journeys 'round the world's jungles and savannahs, arenas and prosceniums. Every stage is haunted, you know."

Including Cinema 12 at the mall? Meaning each of the twelve auditoriums is haunted, or does one ghost work the entire Cineplex?

"Well, sir, you knew her a long time ago. Does she seem . . . different . . . now?"

He considers this. "Halina's mind used to be as clear as the bell atop London's Big Ben. Now, however? I'm not so certain. The fact is, young man, Halina has a flair for the dramatic."

"Well, she's very sure Toibe, her twin sister, is the ghost of Silver Brook."

"Quite impossible, my boy. I know for a fact that

Halina did not, and does not, have a sister of any sort, twin or elsewise."

"Whoa!" That hits me like a gust of winter wind. But then, who *is* Lina hearing through the heating vent? If she's hearing anyone.

19

At home, the tension is thick enough to carve a jack-o'-lantern face. Mom isn't even nagging me to study my bar mitzvah stuff. She used to watch at the window for me to get off the bus so I could tell her about my school day, but now she just calls down from her office in the attic: "That you, Eddie?"

I hear Gabby dancing around, plugged into the iPod that bypasses her ears and blasts music straight into her neurons.

And Dad? He's on the road. His job search takes him farther and farther from home. Last week he was in Tulsa, and this week, Muskogee. If he lands a job there, how will he commute a hundred and forty miles each way?

Wait!

I pound on Gabby's door. She opens it and pulls out one earbud, giving me half her attention.

"What if we have to move to Muskogee?" I yell in her open ear.

"Is that in Oklahoma? Is it even in America?"

"Yeah, it's like a two-hour drive away."

"Problem, working." Her eyes sort of spin like a cyborg's. "Okay, problem solved. We'll go live in a tent in Myriad Gardens." Gabby plugs her other ear.

I almost get my toe out of the way before she slams the door.

On Friday morning, Ms. Perini is kind of spacey, waving her hands around until we notice the flashy ring.

"You got engaged!" Azmara shouts gleefully, and Ms. Perini actually giggles as she nods.

"Great news and congrats and all that," I say, "but we've got a lot of work to do here."

Azmara snaps to attention. "Right! The final tweaks before we take Zippy out for a test run." Her fingers fly over the keys while she barks orders to Joe. I've told them about Mrs. Boniface and how much she could use somebody like Zippy in her life. They're on board with taking Zippy to Silver Brook for a trial. Ms. Perini hasn't given permission yet, though. So far she's only told us not to get ahead of ourselves.

A minute before the bell rings for first period, I ask, "Think we're ready for a field test, Ms. Perini?"

"What? Oh, sure, probably, I guess," she answers while checking out the best spots in the room to catch the light bulbs' glint off her ring. Not exactly an overwhelming vote of confidence, but I'll take it.

20

Monday afternoon, Joe and Azmara and I tumble out of Azmara's mother's car for a group hug—geek version of a football huddle.

"Wait here. I've gotta smooth-talk the administrator or she won't let Zippy and the rest of you in." I scuttle inside, past Lina and past Officer Kinsey, who's lurking behind the reception desk. He's definitely got a thing for Judy.

Ms. Brubaker comes out swinging. "We can*not* have strangers gallivanting all over the place. We have the residents' security to protect."

Me, all sugary: "Aw, please, Ms. Brubaker. It's a special gift for Mrs. Boniface."

"Who is beyond help," Ms. Brubaker retorts. She slaps her hand over her mouth. "You didn't hear me say that. I never said it."

"Said what?" My sweet eyes drill into her.

"Are you blackmailing me?"

"What? I didn't say anything."

"What's your little plan, Eddie?"

Little plan? It's epic! "My robotics squad built a robot, Zippy, who's gonna make Mrs. Boniface so happy that she'll start singing 'Boogie Woogie Bugle Boy of Company B' right along with Mrs. DiAngelo."

Ms. Brubaker looks unconvinced. "That would be a miracle."

"The squad's outside. Please? Here are their names and phone numbers, plus signed permission from our robotics coach."

Ms. Brubaker sighs deeply. "I suppose it won't do any harm." The way she says it, you'd think she was heading to the orthodontist for a maniacal tightening. I know what *that* feels like.

So Azmara and Joe are in, and Ms. Brubaker joins us to cluster around Mrs. Boniface's doorway. Wish we could do this without her, in case it goes haywire.

"Okay, squad," I warn as we approach Mrs. Boniface, "don't crowd the lady. Don't touch her. Just smile a lot."

Poor Mrs. Boniface looks terrified by this onslaught of visitors. Her eyes slide from one of us to the next.

"It's okay, Thelma, these are my friends. This is Joe, and that's Azmara. We have the surprise I promised you."

I nod to Joe, who sets the new, improved Zippy down on her wheels in front of Mrs. Boniface. Zippy is wheelchair height, about the size of your average annoying toddler. "Thelma Boniface, meet your new friend, Zippy!"

Azmara switches Zippy on, and Mrs. Boniface jerks up straight when the blue eyes shine right at her.

We activate voice recognition and response in Zippy's own voice. Eyes fixed on Mrs. Boniface, I speak into the small mic slung around my neck, slow and steady: "ZIPPY, HOW ARE YOU FEELING TODAY?"

Zippy churns a few seconds, then goes, "FUH!" That means *fine* in Robotese.

"Great, because I want you to meet my friend Thelma."

Ms. Brubaker mutters under her breath, "Is this for real?"

Joe pulls Zippy back with computer commands,

and she slides right next to Mrs. Boniface, turned to face her on the side not deadened by the stroke.

"I'll demonstrate, Thelma. See? You talk right into this microphone. Start each sentence with Zippy's name, which activates her response, and make sure to say each syllable in the same flat, unaccented way. It's voice-activation software," I brag, as if I'd invented the technology myself. "Like this: 'ZIPPY, MY NAME IS EDDIE,' only you'd say 'THELMA.'"

Zippy churns and cranks a few seconds. I think Azmara's going to faint before the robot finally says, "ER-ROW," which, if you have an active imagination, sounds like *hello*.

"ZIPPY, I'M FEELING SAD TODAY," I say, and Zippy whimpers, with her voice rising and falling sympathetically.

Mrs. Boniface's eyebrow creeps up, one hair at a time. Is Zippy getting to her?

Zippy says: "ER-ROW. FUH." Hello, fine. Yeah, she's got *those* down. But also, "URRRU?" The question mark is silent but implied: AND YOU?

Mrs. Boniface's one good eye goes round, and half her face frowns, making my heart sink.

Ms. Brubaker is getting restless. She'll pull us any second.

But Mrs. Boniface's shaky, gnarled hand slowly rises from her lap for three slow, soft pats on Zippy's head. Her dry lips part once, twice. No words come out of her rusty throat, but she sure is trying.

The squad beams and high-fives, and Ms. Brubaker actually says, "Astounding."

It's Eddie, one; Brubaker, zip.

"All right, that's enough excitement for Mrs. Boniface for today," Ms. Brubaker says, dismissing Azmara and Joe with a wave of her hand. "In my office, Eddie. We have something to discuss."

Ms. Brubaker unlocks her office door with the key that she keeps on a stretchy cord around her neck. Once we're inside, she closes the door with a soft *ca-ching*. "Sit down, Eddie."

My backpack thuds to the floor, and Flambé yelps even though it landed nowhere near him. I notice that each of the cabinets along the wall has a picture of a dog hanging on it: big poodles standing at attention like marines.

"Yes, my portraits," says Ms. Brubaker. "You see, Flambé is a legacy dog. Those are his parents and siblings, all champion show dogs, like Flambé himself."

But the dog whose picture's attached to the last cabinet has its head buried in its paws. "That one? Ah, that's Flambé's littermate, Dunce, who unfortunately has no talent. That apple has fallen far from the tree."

I'm distracted by a box of chocolate marshmallow bunnies on the desk. My mouth waters, but does Ms. Brubaker offer me one? No. Even Flambé has a treat, crunching away on a rawhide bone, which is starting to look tasty to me.

"As you know," Ms. Brubaker says, "some of our residents have reported things missing, including some items of considerable value. The disappearances began a few short weeks ago. Nothing like this has ever happened here at Silver Brook."

I slump in my chair. *A few short weeks ago* was when I started volunteering.

"I've interviewed our staff. They've all been here for years."

"I'm the only one who's new. Me and Tessa."

"Correct, though Tessa was here before you came, and nothing suspicious happened then." She lets a silence hang between us.

"You think I've been stealing?"

"I don't know what to think, but these thefts are escalating, and we don't know what else people may have lost, since many of them don't remember what they had in the first place."

"I'm no thief!" Flambé stops chomping to look up at me. I'm mad enough to snatch that rawhide out of his mouth, but I'd probably lose three fingers, and then it would be a lot harder to catch at first base.

Hank sticks his head in the door. Feels like he's saying, *I've got your back, kid.* But the actual words are "Want me to check on the guy fixing the leak in the basement?"

"No!" Ms. Brubaker flips her silvery pen, which rolls to the floor. Flambé dodges it. My imagination, or is she super nervous? "He's doing fine, thank you."

Hank tosses me a sympathetic look and closes the door quietly.

"I'm hoping we can resolve this, Eddie. Rabbi Kefler has vouched for you."

My blood's boiling. "You talked to my rabbi about this?"

"Of course. And tomorrow after school I need you to bring one of your parents here with you. Officer Kinsey wants to talk to you."

My heart pounds in my ears. I'm pretty sure Officer Kinsey isn't a real cop, but I can already feel my wrists cuffed to a chain on the table, bright pinpoint lights beaming into my eyes. There'll be a good cop/bad cop combo tricking me into confessing to a crime I didn't commit. Happens all the time on TV. "The security guard's going to interrogate me?"

"Not an interrogation, just some routine questions. So, tomorrow, four o'clock, bring one of your parents. I'll see you then."

I slingshot out of my seat. Flambé marches me to the door. Stomping out, I slam the door behind me so hard that the window rattles.

Dang, I left my backpack in the office! I'm too angry to go back for it. Also, I'd look like a doofus. It would be like if I stole second base, then had to go back to first to pick up my retainer.

21

At dinner, Dad's in a foul mood, stabbing the salad veggies as though they've personally insulted him. A mini tomato flies across the table, and Mom yells, "Jake! Get a grip!"

Not the greatest time to drop the bombshell about the not-a-cop meeting, but I've got no choice. "Mom, Dad, something's up at Silver Brook. Ms. Brubaker—she wants one of you to go over there with me tomorrow."

Gabby flashes me a *what's up?* look.

"What for, honey?" asks Mom

I swallow a gob of spit. "The security guard wants to talk to me."

A hunk of stew on its way to Dad's mouth dangles off his fork. "What's going on, Eddie?"

"Some stuff has disappeared from peoples' rooms."

Smashing a potato wedge on her plate, Mom says, "They can't think you've been stealing from the residents."

"They might think so," I admit. "But I didn't, I swear!"

"I know you didn't. Jake, do you want to go, or should I?"

"We'll both go."

"Me too?" Gabby offers.

"No," the parents say at once.

She pouts. "I never get to have fun. The curse of being the baby in the family."

Dad shoves the meat into his mouth and talks around it, which Gabby and I would get our allowance docked for. "We'll dispense with this quickly tomorrow. Now, let's enjoy your mother's excellent lamb stew," he says grimly.

Like anybody except Gabby has an appetite.

⁂

Officer Kinsey pumps my parents' hands as if they're old army buddies. My eye's on a dark hair that needs to be stuffed back up into his nose. The hair on his head is slicked back with some sort of goo, maybe the stuff he shines his boots with.

Flambé's collar jiggles as he circles his owner's office, stopping at each cabinet to admire his famous relatives.

I grab my backpack, which is sitting right where I left it on the office floor. I had to bluff and apologize my way through school today, and I'll have a double load of homework to catch up on tonight—if I make it out of this meeting in one piece.

Mom, Dad, and I sit across the table from Ms. Brubaker and Officer Kinsey. Hey, three of us only two of them. We got 'em!

"Mr. and Mrs. Lewin, thank you for coming in during your busy workday," says Ms. Brubaker.

Dad flinches. *What workday?* "Why do you suspect my son?" he demands.

Officer Kinsey answers. "We're interviewing staff, volunteers, and residents alike, Mr. Lewin."

Mom asks, "Do we need a lawyer?"

"You're jumping to conclusions, ma'am." Officer Kinsey's Adam's apple bobs up and down, loose in his throat. "Everybody stay cool."

Dad hasn't been *cool* since he quit his job.

"A few questions, Ed." I want to say *Nobody calls me Ed*, but this doesn't seem like the ideal time to bring that up. "Do you have free access to residents' premises?"

"Well, I don't have a key card, so I can't go into their apartments on my own."

"But their doors are often open."

"Well, yeah. But I never go in unless they invite me."

"Do they give verbal consent?"

Except Thelma Boniface, who's never verbal. "Mostly."

Ms. Brubaker clears her throat. "Eddie is like a pet around here."

Arf. Roll over, play dead. Flambé is eyeing me snobbishly, as if to say, *You are not my equal.*

"Where are you going with this, officer?" Dad snaps.

"Hold your horses, Mr. Lewin. I'm just saying that it's possible for *any person* who's gained the residents' trust to get access to the residents' personal property. I understand that Mrs. Boniface has a special relationship with you, son."

"I talk to her, read to her sometimes."

"Commendable. Ed, do you get an allowance?"

Mom jumps in to keep Dad from going ballistic. "Fifteen dollars a week for snacks, a dollar for charity at Hebrew School. About what his friends get."

Kinsey's smile shows no teeth. Maybe he keeps his mouth shut to stop his Adam's apple from escaping. "I've got a daughter about your boy's age, and there's always stuff she wants. Is fifteen dollars enough to cover your expenses, son?"

Dad flares again. "You're insinuating that Eddie steals to supplement his allowance. I resent that implication!"

"Jake." Mom strokes Dad's hand.

He's embarrassing me, making me *feel* guilty. What if he blurts out that he lost his job? That we're cutting back on things—dinners out, new clothes, my bar mitzvah party? That would make me look more desperate, more like a thief.

Officer Kinsey leans forward, folds his hands on the table. "You play sports, Ed?"

"Baseball, sir. First base."

"Commendable." He sits back in his chair. "Ever been in trouble, son? Ever done things you didn't get caught for, like clipping a pack of gum at the store, or slipping a package of baseball cards into your hoodie pocket?"

"No, sir."

"Commendable." His favorite word. "I understand you're here on a volunteer program at your church."

"Synagogue," Mom corrects him. "Community service is a requirement for his bar mitzvah."

"We've had many bar and bat mitzvah students here in the past. Never any trouble like this," says Ms. Brubaker.

"Well, Ms. Brubaker, here's what I'm gonna suggest. Ed here's a nice kid, and I wouldn't want to interfere in his—what did you call it?—bar mitzvoo project? So, son, I'll let you keep on coming here for the time being, but stay out of residents' apartments. Keep your nose clean, and I'll keep my ears open and an eye on you, and no mouthing off to anybody, got it?"

Which pretty much covers all the parts of a face except the zits.

22

Gabby leaps on me at the door. "I'm dying to know how it went."

How should I answer her? I can't admit that I'm scared I'll get thrown in the youth detention center. Is there a visiting day? How long will I last in juvie?

What I say is, "It went okay, except Dad lost his cool. Hope he finds work soon, because he's sure on a short fuse."

"For real! He snapped my head off about turning my music down. They're worried sick about money. What about you? Are you worried, Eddie?"

"About people thinking I'm the Silver Brook burglar? Nah." I toss it off lightly, but my knees are knocking like a pair of dice. I'm not off the hook yet, not judging by the way Kinsey stared at me with his jumpy Adam's apple ready to jettison out of his mouth and smack me in the eye. "The security guy didn't haul me off to juvie in shackles, or even stop me from doing my mitzvah project."

"Well, if you need help with your alibi, I'm willing to work pro bono."

"I'll let you know." It's a pain in the butt to have a little sister who's a genius, especially when I'm not one. But she's on my side. She'll visit me in juvie and bring me news of the outside world.

An earthquake of fear shudders through me. It could set seismographic records.

But suddenly I come to my senses. I'm not the Silver Brook burglar. They can't pin it on me with no evidence, no way. No way.

Can they?

I bring Tessa up to speed on my status as the prime suspect in the Silver Brook burglary case.

"Well, we'll just have to do a little detective work to clear your name," she says. "There's got to be evidence implicating the real criminal. As soon as we find that, you're off the hook."

We head to the basement to check the spy cam.

Not for ghosts—I'm looking for a living, breathing burglar.

Let's face it. We built the thing from a thirty-dollar kit. The FBI and CIA won't be begging to borrow it for surveillance out in the field. But it *does* have a motion detector on it and—hey—someone's been moving around down here! I download the measly twelve seconds of sped-up video to my phone. The cam sweep of the room shows a fuzzy guy between the fifty-five-gallon paint cans, with his back to the camera, so all I make out is a bunch of tools in the pockets of a leather apron hanging over his butt.

Aw, it's nobody, just the plumber working on one of the leaks that always seem to be popping up.

Back upstairs, we try alternative tactics—until, fifteen minutes before the end of my volunteer slot, Ms. Brubaker summons me to her office again.

Could Ms. Brubaker pick a more uncomfortable chair to park me in across from her desk? I shift around to find a non-itchy spot on the wooly seat. Wooden ladder slats cut into my back.

"You wanted to talk to me?"

"Eddie, one of the residents who shall go nameless said you were snooping around in Mrs. Callahan's apartment, after Officer Kinsey expressly asked you not to go into residents' living spaces."

I feel my face redden, which makes my freckles pop out like measles. "Mrs. Callahan asked me to pull her hat boxes down off her closet shelf, so while I was there . . ."

"You inspected for stolen goods. Very enterprising. What did you find?"

"Nothing! I mean, nothing that didn't belong to her." The only weird things were six stamped envelopes addressed to Silver Brook Pavilion, which made me wonder why she'd be addressing letters to herself. "And I put everything back on the shelf."

"Naturally." The smile on Ms. Brubaker's face has icicles dripping from it. "What were you doing in Mrs. DiAngelo's apartment?"

Sheesh, does some secret agent report every step I take? Probably it's Fake-Cop Kinsey. Maybe he built his own spy cam. *Commendable.* I'm so nervous that my legs and feet wind tight around each other, like two boa constrictors in love. My toes will be dead meat. I'll be thumping out of here on my knees.

"Mrs. DiAngelo showed me her wedding album." Which I've seen twenty times already, until every purple page is limp. "So, while I was there . . ." I catch myself biting my thumbnail and quickly tuck it under my leg.

"You snooped." She makes it sound tacky. "I appreciate your *amateur* detective efforts, Eddie, but you have to understand how it looks from my perspective. Questionable. Suspicious."

"I know, but . . ."

"If you plan to complete your mitzvah project, starting today, you will not enter anyone's apartment unless one of our *trusted* staff members is with you. Is that clear?"

"Totally. But—"

"And no more visits from your school friends and their little robot until this is cleared up."

"But—"

"That will be all, Eddie. Have a nice day."

23

I stop by Silver Brook after school on Friday. Yeah, Friday's not my day, and Ms. Brubaker will probably think my presence is *questionable*, but I want to check the spy cam. My cover story is that I'm bringing Mrs. DiAngelo some purple grapes to keep her going through the weekend.

"You're a kind boy. There are green grapes and red grapes, you know, but those are not as beautiful as these," she says, spitting seeds into a potted plant in the dayroom.

"See you on Monday, Mrs. D."

Nothing new on the spy cam. The cook's been down here a few times for giant cans of peaches and applesauce, and the cleaning crew grabs supplies, but nobody's done anything suspicious.

Before I leave, I head to Mrs. Boniface's room

for a quick check-in. "Hi, Thelma. Zippy says hello." Or would, if Zippy had an actual brain. I don't tell Mrs. Boniface that Zippy's been banned from the premises until further notice. That's just one more reason the Silver Brook burglar needs to get caught.

Behind me, I hear Hank's keys jangling. How come they all of a sudden sound like jailers' keys? I turn to see him coming down the hall toward us. "How's it going, Eddie? Didn't think you'd be here today."

"Just a quick visit," I say. "Don't worry, I'm not going anywhere I'm not supposed to."

"Sounds good. I know firsthand how easy it can be to get attached to folks here. But the boss would probably prefer it if you stick to your assigned days."

"Sure, Hank. No problem." I turn to Mrs. Boniface. "Gotta run, Thelma. Have a good weekend." Which is like every other day in her monotonous world. I can't help wondering who sends those mysterious payments to keep her at Silver Brook but never bothers coming to visit.

On my way out, I pass Lina in the lobby and do a double take. She's wearing a wrinkled, sweat-stained baseball cap that looks as if it's been stashed away in an attic for fifty years. Her mustard-colored hair sticks out the hole in the back of the cap like a stubby shock of wheat.

The ball cap looks familiar . . . that big red *B*, outlined in white, which means Boston. Red Sox! Ohhhh, maybe *that's* why she wears those filthy red things on her feet, so ragged that her yellowed big toenail pokes out of a hole.

"Nice ball cap, Lina. I'm heading home. Shabbat shalom."

"Shabbos, we had no candles. At first, yes, little stubs we lit and blew out for next week. Then, all the candles were gone. Wine? *Pfft!* We were lucky to have water, not even clean."

I know I shouldn't ask. "Where was that, Lina?"

"You wouldn't want to know."

Against my own advice—*Eddie, stay out of it!*—I ask, "Was your twin sister, Toibe, there?"

"Where else would she be?"

Lina's watching me with a face that's—how can I say this?—haunted. Her eyes are sunken, her lips quiver like she's freezing.

"Lina, are you okay?"

She takes off the ball cap and rakes her hands

through her flattened hair until it stands up in straw peaks, and she says, "Half the time you don't make sense."

Ugh, why did I even bother? "*I* don't make sense? I'm not the one who hears my dead sister talking to me through the heating vent in, oh yeah, a man's voice. Where's the sense in that, huh, Lina?" I twirl around. "Come on out, Toibe, wherever you are. Show us your ghostly face."

"She's hiding in the cellar."

"What? You mean the basement here at Silver Brook?"

"The cellar. No food, no water. The lady can only take one."

"What lady?"

"Jadziya, the Polish girl."

Oh, man, I'm not following any of this, but I shouldn't have lost my patience with her, so I squat down beside her wheelchair. Phew, those socks! "Lina? Lemme guess: you're sad that you're alive and your twin sister died, right? A long time ago?"

She rears back, as if I've said *Pardon me, but your nose just fell into your oatmeal.*

"Yesterday," she insists.

"I don't get it."

"Ignoramus. Ask your rabbi friend." She grabs the big wheels of her chair and carves a path around me.

"Wait!" I feel awful for making fun of her, for being sarcastic, for upsetting her even more. There must be a way to make it up to her. "You're a Red Sox fan, aren't you?"

She pauses and works her hair back into the ball cap. "Isn't everyone?"

"Red Sox, meh. I like the Houston Astros."

"Never heard of 'em."

Of course not. She hasn't heard of anything in the twenty-first century. "Okay, how come you like the Red Sox?"

"Because I came *this close* to marrying Yaz."

"Carl Yastrzemski? For real?"

"Have you ever known me to kid around?" Her eyes go fuzzy. "Such a dreamboat. Coal-back hair, smoldering dark brown eyes, that chin, oh the chin on him. Of course, he had quite a honker. He was batting .321 in 1963."

This she remembers, but ask her apartment number? Forget it!

"Up at the plate, my Yaz, he held his bat sky-high like nobody else. Tough on the pitcher."

"So, why didn't you marry him?"

Her piercing look shouts that I must be an idiot to ask. "Yastrzemski and Kempinski? Our two names wouldn't even fit on a wedding invitation. Anyways, he was already married to a girl with a nice, short name. Carol somebody."

"You've had a pretty dramatic life, Lina."

"You could say that."

"Listen, since you're a big baseball fan, you want to come with my family to a game?"

"Not if it's those Houston Ashcans."

"No, it's my school team, the Oakridge Oilers."

"*Pfft*, bush league. I'll think about it." She flicks the cap's bill.

"We'll pick you up at four o'clock next Thursday afternoon. But you gotta change your socks. We're blue and gold."

The next week is quiet. No new thefts, but I'm still under surveillance. Hank's been assigned to keep an eye on me at all times, like the guy doesn't have enough to do. I have to rely on Tessa to check the spy cam, which still hasn't coughed up any leads, and to keep her eyes open when she gets a chance to check out some of the residents' apartments.

I stick to the common areas, where there's plenty for me to do: help Earl Archer figure out how to use his new phone, look at Mrs. DiAngelo's wedding album with her again, referee Maurie and Herman's arguments, and wonder what it's going to be like to take Lina to a baseball game.

24

You can't exactly check a person out like a library book. At Silver Brook's front desk, Judy has Dad sign forms saying we won't kidnap Lina and hold her for ransom and that we're responsible if she's knocked out in a fight on the ball field or bopped by a wild pitch.

While Flambé supervises from inside the building, Mom and Dad and Gabby and I load Lina, her walker, her wheelchair, her emergency oxygen tank, her floppy sunbonnet, her afternoon meds, a half-pint carton of orange juice in case she goes into diabetic shock, ID stuff on a thumb drive, and a baggie full of goldfish crackers that she can suck on even without her teeth. Also her teeth, in a blue plastic box like I keep my retainer in at night.

Flambé cries pitifully as we shut the van door. He wants to escape with us.

At the ballpark, Lina positions her chair along the first base line. When the ump shouts, "Lady, back up before you get beaned," she rolls back a few spins, then inches closer to the chalk again, shouting color commentary on every play.

She taunts Emanuel, our pitcher: "Come on, you've got a bazooka arm, kid. Throw an Uncle Charlie curveball. Throw strikes! Right down Broadway, that-a-boy!"

It's worse when we're batting, especially when I come up to the plate. "Here comes the pitch, kid. That's a meatball, get some lumber on it. Hit it where they ain't out there. Let's see a three-bagger, right past the hot corner!" When the ump dares to call, "Stee-rike!" Lina hollers, "You call that a strike? You're blind as a bat. Here, take my glasses."

Ump calls for a time-out. "Kid, get your grandma off my field. She's a public nuisance."

She's wheeled back to the bleachers, and Dad locks her chair in place while Gabby blocks the wheels with crushed Pepsi cans.

Hey, we win the game. How could we lose with Lina as our cheerleader?

On the way back to Silver Brook, she says, "That's the most fun I've had since the Hula-Hoop was invented in the fifties."

So now we're buddies all of a sudden.

※ ※ ※

Monday afternoon, Lina's sitting in her wheelchair on the front porch. No red socks, no ball cap. Her eyes seem shrunken.

"Hey, Lina. My baseball coach says hi. He's wondering if you're interested in a side gig as our team mascot."

No response. "Lina?" I snap my fingers near her nose. "You there?" I'm not sure she is, because her eyes are fixed on something way past me. Did she have a seizure? A stroke?

Maybe I should reintroduce myself, like the handbook suggests. "It's me—Eddie. We went to a baseball game, remember?"

"Who are you looking for?"

"For you! Lina. Halina Kempinski."

She shakes her head and says in a small, feeble voice, "I am Rivke, but I must never, ever tell anyone." Her face sinks in, blotched and red, and her eyes swim with tears. "Promise me you won't tell?"

"Um, okay."

She clutches my wrist. "Promise me, and I will talk to you, only you. Promise!"

"I promise," I say, though I'm not sure what I'm promising. "But I don't get it. What's wrong?"

"You don't understand. You have to understand. You have to."

I'm in way over my head here, so I press Lina's help button. As soon as Lupita comes, I whisper, "She's really upset. I don't know what to do."

"The rabbi," says Lina. Her voice is shaky, and her accent's getting stronger. "Have him come here. He knows. He can help me explain."

I call Rabbi Kefler, hoping he really can help make sense of this.

He must have driven like a maniac, because he rushes into Silver Brook twenty minutes later, in such a hurry that he clunks his head on the glass door before it can slide open.

Lupita is waiting in the dayroom with Lina. The other seniors have all gone to the dining hall, so there's nobody else around. I'm a deactivated robot, afraid to say a word to Lina, while the rabbi steers me into one of the chairs near her. Lupita steps out of the room to give us privacy.

Lina says to the rabbi, "I want to tell him. The boy from baseball. I want him to know."

Rabbi Kefler says, "All right. Go ahead. It's safe. You can tell him. I'll just sit right here, and you talk to Eddie."

She mumbles something I can't make out and jerks her hands up to rake her fingers through her hair.

It all feels heavy, important.

Rabbi Kefler says, "Maybe you can start by telling him your name."

"Halina Kempinski," she replies flatly.

"Your real name."

"I cannot! I promised Jadziya."

"Yes, you can," he says soothingly. "You're safe here."

"Mama . . . Papa . . ."

"They're no longer living, are they?"

Seems cruel to say that, but Rabbi's eyes and voice are kind. It's so quiet in this room that I can hear air whistling up my nose.

"Eddie, ask her to tell you her name." What, he forgot it?

"What's your name?" I ask, and the rabbi whispers to me, "Her name is Rivke Koplowicz."

I'm clueless, but I follow his lead. "Is your name Rivke Koplowicz?"

"No! That is a Jewish name. I have a Christian name. I am a Pole, not a Jew." Her voice is as shrill as a fire engine.

Rabbi leans in a little closer to her. "You are Rivke Koplowicz. Your mother and father were Basra and Yitzak. Your sister—"

"No, no, I have no sister!"

"Rivke, your sister was Toibe. She did not survive."

Suddenly Lina—Rivke—starts jabbering in another language, probably Yiddish or Polish, which the rabbi doesn't understand any better than I do.

She gulps down two cups full of water from the tray on the table, and Rabbi Kefler says, "Do you want to explain to Eddie what we're talking about, Rivke? Are you ready?"

And the story pours out in English now, faster than water from the pitcher. And it's like nothing I've ever heard or imagined.

25

"Always we are cold, even summer," Lina begins, in that tiny voice. "Cold because always we are hungry . . ."

Rabbi Kefler explains the unexplainable to me in a calm, quiet way. "Warsaw, Poland, World War II, under German occupation. Some four hundred thousand Jews were forced into a ghetto behind a ten-foot wall, trying to survive on fewer calories a day than you'd feed a cat."

The Holocaust. I've heard about it; who hasn't? My great-grandpa was a liberator of one of the death camps. Which one? I never thought to ask him while he was alive.

"We are glad for a shred of meat, half a rotten potato," she says. "Sometimes, a good Pole—even once, twice, a German—smuggles food to us.

An apple. Ten ways we divide it, even the seeds."

My stomach knots. Guilt pings me for every time I've said, *What's for dinner, Mom? I'm starving.*

"We are seven, eight to a room, no privacy even to pish. Every day, more dead. A wagon comes to carry away the bodies after people take their ragged clothes or boots for warmth, or to sell for a few more bites of bread or medicine or a stick of wood to burn."

"Rivke, tell Eddie something fine in the middle of all the horror."

She doesn't answer for a long time. "Fine—yes. We have secret schools, hospitals, shuls, I heard even once a nightclub. We keep going, Shabbos after Shabbos. Children as small as me, they are spies to tell when the guard sleeps. They sneak through tunnels, through holes in the wall, and bring back food or medicine. Mama gives it all to us. And Jadziya, the Polish girl . . ." Her eyes light up. "She brings us what will keep us alive, and she carries out babies in her toolbox, sometimes a laundry sack, to give to Polish families, so we won't die in the ghetto. We are twins, Toibe and me. Not the same alike. Toibe is big-boned, like Papa, though God knows on her bones there is no meat. I also am skin and bones, but shrunken, the size of a baby, barely walking."

The big Thanksgiving turkey she told me about. Her voice is hollow. "Mama is crying, pushing me into Jadziya's arms and pulling me back until Jadziya grabs my shoulder, pulls me away from Mama. *You are no more Rivke Koplowicz,* Jadziya tells me. *Starting this minute, you are Halina Kempinski, a Polish girl. Say it, child. Halina Kempinski. Again. A soldier asks you, What is your name, little girl? You answer, Halina Kempinski.* To Mama, she promises, *I will find you after the war. You and your daughter will see each other again,* and I am still saying over and over *Halina Kempinski* when she stuffs me into her toolbox, so tight I cannot move my legs. A heel is in my mouth. Before she clasps shut the box, she tells Mama, *Tomorrow I will come back for your other girl. I have a Polish family willing to take twins. Tomorrow.*" But tomorrow Mama and Papa and Toibe are on a cattle car going to Treblinka."

Rabbi Kefler half-reaches for her hand, which she pulls back to her lap. I grind my teeth to fight back tears, and Rabbi Kefler drapes his arm over my shoulders.

And now Lina finds her regular voice. "Toibe, she has never forgiven me. Every day of my life, she reminds me. When I tell you she is pure evil, I mean what happened to her—that is evil. And that is what survives of her, what will not let me have peace." She takes another gulp of water.

After that, what can we say? Anybody else, we'd give her a reassuring hug, but Lina's made it clear she doesn't want to be touched.

"Thank you for trusting us with this, Lina," Rabbi Kefler says finally. "If you ever want to talk more, I'll be here. So will Eddie."

He nods for us to wheel Lina back to her sentry post by the front door where she's most comfortable. Rabbi Kefler talks to Lupita for a minute, and afterward we quietly leave Lina.

Outside, Rabbi Kefler says, "Eddie, go home and tell your parents about all this. Call if you want to talk to me later."

In a total daze, I walk home, trusting muscle memory to get me across the street before a car speeds around the corner. We've got one of those keypads for the garage door, which is the way I usually get in, but suddenly I can't remember the code. I'm not sure I'd remember my own name if anyone asked me. I punch random numbers until the code finally comes to my fingers. I'm relieved to see both cars in the garage, and Gabby's bike is gone. This time calls for a kid and both his parents alone, more than any other time.

I burst into the kitchen, where Mom and Dad are discussing a stack of bills. "We've gotta talk about the Holocaust."

They clunk their coffee cups down. Mom's face drains of all color. They listen as I pour out everything Lina said, everything Rabbi Kefler explained, everything I *don't* know about what happened in those way-off places, way back then. Until today, the 1940s seemed like centuries ago.

We talk for two hours, more time than I've spent talking to my parents in the last three years combined, except when I had my tonsils out and pain meds turned me into a running faucet of words that I thought were hilarious and that gave Mom a blazing headache. This time, I'm the one aching. Not a headache—a heartache.

Mom tells me again about her grandfather, who was part of the American forces that liberated one of the Nazi camps. And Dad tells me about his great-uncle Shlomo, a kid not much older than I am when he escaped the Warsaw ghetto, like Lina. He survived in a frozen Polish forest, a bunch of dead tree limbs and twigs his only blanket.

This hits home. It's about *my* family, *my* people. Six million of them killed, and a million of those were kids. Another six million died too—Poles, Slavs, gay people, disabled people, anyone who didn't fit into the Nazis' idea of a superior human. It's staggering to hear numbing numbers like this. And to suddenly feel so much closer to it all, so connected to it.

"Nothing like that could ever happen again, could it?"

My parents are both quiet, until finally Dad answers: "It's your responsibility, Eddie. Yours, mine, every decent human's, to make sure it doesn't."

26

Jogging up the ramp to Silver Brook on Wednesday, I'm wondering what I'm going to say to Lina. She's probably as embarrassed to face me as I am to see her after that raw, super-intense time. Do I apologize? What for—the Nazis who killed her family, the neighbors who let it happen? Do I go all mushy and squat down next to her wheelchair and tell her how heartbreaking it all is? Or do I just dive into the latest baseball news as if nothing happened? But something *has* happened; we're changed. I can't unhear what she told me, or unfeel it.

She's at her usual place, and when the door swooshes open, she says, "It's four fifteen, you're late."

"I had a Robotics Club thing."

"Typical. Your generation is always overcommitted."

Same old Lina. Why was I worried?

"Sorry to keep you waiting, Lina. *Or . . . do you want me to call you Rivke now?*"

"Nonsense. I've been Lina for eighty years, so stick with that, Eddie Whatever. In here, though?" She taps her chest. "In here I'm Rivke."

<hr />

As usual, Mrs. Boniface slumps in the doorway of her apartment. I know I'm not allowed to go in, but I have to at least check up on her.

"Hi, Thelma. Do you have anything you want me to tell Zippy?" Not that I expect Mrs. Boniface to answer—but she does, kind of. Half her face smiles weakly; one eye is pulled closed.

"Well, we'll bring her back to see you again soon." I hope.

Mrs. Boniface tilts her head toward a sound rumbling through the wall—no, from her heating vent.

"Is that a radio?"

Her one good eyebrow rises—her form of a question mark. Or is it an answer?

The words are muffled, but something comes through clearly: "Swell-elegant." Where have I heard that before?

I'm meandering back to the lobby, still stuck on the voice in the heating vent, when the plumber comes around the corner. He's a bulky middle-aged guy loaded down with a tool bag that drags his jeans practically to the danger zone. I dodge him as he almost barrels into me while muttering into a phone that's swallowed up in his giant palm.

"Moved? How come? Got it, yeah, Ekroo."

Ekroo must be the name of the person he's talking to, probably a staff member I haven't met yet?

An idea socks me between the eyes. Ms. Brubaker told me that none of the Silver Brook staff are under suspicion for the thefts because they've all worked here for years. But what about that new person, Ekroo? Or the plumber himself. He's been coming around a lot for the last few weeks.

He disappears down the hallway as Tessa cuts across the lobby toward me. "Mrs. DiAngelo has been looking for you, Lewin. You hiding out?"

"Hey, Tessa, do you know a staff member around here named Ekroo? Could be a first name or a last name."

"Why?"

"The plumber was talking to somebody by that name, maybe somebody new on the staff. I'm wondering if Ekroo could be the Silver Brook burglar."

"Ekroo sounds like a skin disease, the evil twin of acne."

"Wait, maybe it's not a name. Maybe it's a thing." A thing that means something to my newest suspect.

She whips out her phone and thumbs in *e-k-r-o-o*. "It's a town in Mississippi. A type of baby gown from the Philippines. Also a company that makes pants, only it's spelled *E-c-r-u*."

"Forget it. None of that makes sense." Still, it bounces around in my mind.

⁂

The dinner bell rings. In the stampede to the dining room, Maurie and Herman are having a fight.

"Place I used to live had some pizzazz. Wallpaper, fat red zinnias, not like this." Maurie stabs the wall with one of his walking sticks.

"Big dill. They kicked you out of that place with the wallpaper."

"So I'm stuck here"—another stab—"with these sickly beige walls."

"They're not beige, they're ivory."

"Ivory-shmivory, they're beige, dull, mind-numbing."

Tessa and I hide snickers until Mrs. Callahan passes the men and says, "Quit your squabbling, you old coots. The wall color's ecru."

My elbow rams into Tessa's waist at the same time that she socks my arm and says, "Never thought of ecru being a paint color!"

We weave past the seniors, through the kitchen to the basement. No sign of the plumber—he must've worked fast.

One of the paint drums down here has a smear brushed across the label, the same color as the walls upstairs. It's called . . . Ecru Enamel.

"Why would the plumber need to know about a paint can?" I ask Tessa.

To get to Ecru Enamel, we have to roll away three other industrial-sized paint cans that are about half my height and weight, which takes approximately every muscle in my body.

But Ecru Enamel is lighter than the others, and it rattles as we tilt it and roll it a few inches away from the other drums.

Tessa's face lights up. "You thinking what I'm thinking? That the plumber is the thief, and he's stashed the stolen goods in this paint drum?"

"I don't know," I say. "Why would he hide things here instead of just smuggling them out of the building?"

"Unless he didn't bring them down here," says Tessa. "Maybe someone else did. An accomplice on the inside."

"Yeah! Someone lifts stuff off the residents and stashes it down here. Then he collects it from this hiding spot when he comes here to do plumbing jobs. Then maybe he sells the stuff—fences it—and splits the cash with his partner."

"Who could be anyone," Tessa points out. "So, let's see what's in Ecru Enamel!"

But when we pry off the lid, we're staring into a mostly empty cylinder lined with a crusty layer of paint. I spot a roll of green bubble wrap, a short-handled shovel, a rusty hatchet, and a hand broom and dustpan.

"It's just a bunch of random tools," Tessa says,

popping a few green bubbles.

"Maybe." I can feel my brow tighten. "But I still think we're on to something big."

We adjust the position of our hidden spy cam so that it's aimed directly at Ecru Enamel.

"Next we investigate the plumber," I say, and Tessa agrees.

27

"Matt Bowers, from Penn Street Plumbing," Hank says when I ask. "We used to have a different guy, but Matt's been coming around for the last couple of months. You got a plumbing problem, Eddie?"

"My mom. A leak under the kitchen sink. What's his number?"

"Nobody uses phone books anymore—sad." He talks to Siri.

"I thought you'd have his number in your contacts."

"Naw, Ms. Brubaker always calls him. Here it is. Hand me your phone." He adds Matt Bowers to my contact list.

At that moment, chaos breaks loose. Earl Archer flies out of his apartment hollering up and down the hall. "My money for Rebecca's ring! Gone! A grand. Ten big ones!"

The Silver Brook burglar strikes again! This is getting intense.

While Ms. Brubaker, Lupita, and Tessa calm Mr. Archer down, I slip into the one-iMac lab and call Penn Street Plumbing.

No such place, and the number's out of order.

So who's Matt Bowers? And if he is sneaking stolen items out of Silver Brook, who's planting them in the basement for him to collect? I'm trying to piece details together like a big Lego village, but they won't interlock.

Tessa taps me on the shoulder. "I told Mr. Archer you'd show him how to use the maps feature on his phone. That seemed to make him feel a little better. If you've got that covered, I'm going to watch *Law & Order* reruns with the Goldfarbs. Can't wait to hear his comments."

That's when I remember where I've heard the term *swell-elegant*. From Mrs. Goldfarb. She said it was what her husband would say, if he could speak. But the voice Mrs. Boniface and I heard from the room next door wasn't Mrs. Goldfarb's. It was definitely a man, like Lina hears on the other side of the Goldfarbs' apartment—Toibe talking to her in a man's voice.

Connect the dots: either Mrs. Goldfarb has a boyfriend (hah!) or . . . or . . . mute old Mr. Goldfarb speaks!

＊＊＊

I have to leave at five, while Tessa's still hanging out with the Goldfarbs. She's putting in two hours each Wednesday so that she'll finish her mitzvah project on time. I text her as I'm walking home.

Me: Big news!

Tessa: You're going into the Baseball Hall of Fame?

Me: Not that big, but close. Ready for this? Mr. Goldfarb talks.

Tessa: !!! Evidence?

Me: The voice Lina's been hearing through the vent. It might be his.

Tessa: Whoa! But if he can talk, why do he and Mrs. G pretend he can't?

Me: Working on figuring that out. Stand by for updates.

28

"Rabbi, you visit the Goldfarbs at Silver Brook, right?" I ask him on Tuesday before the other b'nai mitzvah kids straggle in. I figure that after our conversation with Lina, Rabbi Kefler's not gonna keep secrets from me. "What do you know about them?"

"Very little, Eliahu. They came here a few months ago from Hoboken, New Jersey, after Mr. Goldfarb's stroke, to be near their grandson's family. Jeremy, in next year's bar mitzvah class, is their great-grandson. Why do you ask?"

"Guess I'm a spy, like in my Torah portion."

Google, work your magic. There are still ten minutes until class starts, enough time for me to pull up a browser window on my phone, tap *Goldfarb Hoboken* into the search bar, and score about fifty hits: Isaac, Rachel, Manny, Ming Toy, Anastasia . . . No Sidney, no Ruth.

Jeremy Goldfarb grandparents. Nothing. Maybe Jeremy has a different last name. Or it's a second marriage for the Goldfarbs. Nah, they've been married sixty-eight years, like she said.

There's one sixth-grade Jeremy in the Hebrew school yearbook, Jeremy Kleinfeld. He *does* have a different last name from his great-grandparents. I key in *Kleinfeld Sidney Hoboken* and out pop twelve hits, cross-referenced with *Kleinfeld Ruth Hoboken.* Bingo! A match. A wedding anniversary picture, their fiftieth. Is that sweet old couple flying under a fake name? Zooming in on the photo, I wouldn't even recognize them.

Wait, this picture was taken two years ago. The math doesn't compute. Different Ruth and Sidney, and Phase I of my research dead-ends. Phase II: Get friendly with Jeremy Kleinfeld.

Only one guy shows up with hair hanging over his eyes when I stake out the sixth-grade classroom.

"Hey, Jeremy, my name's Eddie."

"Yeah? So?"

"I know your great-grandparents." He gives me a curled-lip look, like *This weirdo hangs out with people in their nineties?*

"Yeah, you guessed it, my mitzvah project is at Silver Brook. Isn't that where your greats live?"

"Bessie and Louie? Yeah."

Whoa! *Bessie and Louie?* What about Ruth and Sidney? Better tread carefully here. "They're a cute couple."

He tosses his hair back. "I guess."

"For old folks. Cracks me up the way she talks for him."

"He doesn't say much."

Much? He's quieter than snow.

Jeremy edges into the classroom. "See ya." Probably wondering why this seventh-grade weirdo is bugging him. If an eighth grader was up in my face like that, I'd run, for sure.

Back home, on my laptop, I key in *Bessie Louie Kleinfeld Hoboken* and plow through a lot of nowhere sites, until suddenly, there they are in Kool-Aid colors. It's a picture of their sixty-fifth anniversary, her in a red sparkly dress with a blingy thing around her neck, and him like a penguin in a red bow tie.

Stone-faced Mr. Goldfarb standing tall, grinning ear to ear? Three years have changed him that much? Mrs. Goldfarb said he had a stroke; that could do it. But if he's secretly able to talk while pretending he can't, the stroke story starts to look more questionable.

I dig deeper into the Google vault, until suddenly, something sends me vibrating like a plucked guitar string.

29

Louis Kleinfeld was *famous* around Hoboken. He was like Prince Charles to old Queen Elizabeth, heir to the throne. Only the guy who sat on the throne was Velvel the Balabos.

Google tells me *velvel* means "wolf" and *balabos*, "boss." So Velvel Kleinfeld, Louie's dad, was what the mob would call a wise guy, the boss, the godfather! And Louie was next in line to head the Hoboken Jewish mob.

I didn't know there was a Jewish mob.

But there it is, in black and white: a bunch of old-time 1920s and 1930s guys in Al Capone suits, into bootlegging, extortion, gambling, and loan sharking. A gang called Murder, Inc. headquartered at Rosie Gold's Brooklyn candy store. They called her Midnight Rose because she had all these

Italian and Jewish hitmen dropping by between jobs every night.

My mind's churning as I meet mob bosses like Lepke Buchalter and Joe "The Greaser" Rosenzweig and Benjamin "Bugsy" Siegel and Meyer Lansky (who packed a lot of fierceness into his five-foot-tall body) and Mother Fredericka Mandelbaum, fencer of stolen goods for the mob. A mother mobster!

Here's the notorious Purple Gang in Detroit—man, Mrs. DiAngelo would flip out over them. They're named for the color of rotten meat, and they were rotten to the bone. When liquor was outlawed during Prohibition in the 1920s, Jewish guys imported it from other countries. A juicy fact: underworld bosses, godfathers like Velvel, were sometimes called Rabbi, because rabbis could legally get wine for kiddush in the synagogue. Suddenly in the '20s and '30s, fake "synagogues" popped up along the east coast.

And what's this? A crook named Arnold Rothstein set up eight Chicago White Sox players to throw the 1919 World Series. Okay, mobsters can fool around with extortion and bootlegging, but mess with baseball? That's stepping over the line of decency!

In 1927, Louis Kleinfeld was born smack into

dirty dealings like this in small-time Hoboken. By the time he was twenty years old, he was known as Louie the Lung. With some digging, I find out it's because every time he got caught for a criminal act, his tuberculosis conveniently flared up. A crafty mob lawyer would get him booked into a sanitarium in the mountains for "the cure." Two months later, he'd be out and working his regular gigs. But all that was in the 1940s and early '50s when the Jewish mob was fading into history. As Mr. Caliberti would say, long time ago, long time.

As for Mrs. Goldfarb, Bessie Kleinfeld, she may be a cookie-baking bubbie now, but back in her youth, she was called Bad News Bessie! She and Louie were high school sweethearts in Hoboken, already pulling off heists before they were seniors the *first* time around. She'd come around swinging a baseball bat when she collected on loans. Jeremy's great-grandma must have had quite an arm on her. Could have been a pitcher. I am totally eating this stuff up.

Once the mob started going into decline, Louie and Bessie got out of the game—and out of the whole East Coast. I guess their options were to disappear or wind up in federal prison. The son of the wise guy made a wise decision.

Sheesh, does Jeremy know about his great-grand-parents' shady past? Does *anyone* know that Silver Brook is the latest hideout for these notorious gangsters? Nobody would look for them in an old folks' home in plain old Oklahoma. It's like they're in the witness protection program, only they're the ones innocent people usually have to hide from. They're on the lam, masquerading as a sweet, decrepit old couple. Hiding in plain sight. Hey, maybe Mrs. Goldfarb keeps Mr. Goldfarb quiet so he won't blurt out the wrong thing and blow their cover.

And my job is to rip off their masks. To prove that Sidney and Ruth Goldfarb are really Louie the Lung and Bad News Bessie. Because, hey, with a history like that, they gotta be the Silver Brook burglars!

30

Tessa, with her freshly blue-striped hair hanging over her shoulder, meets me in front of Silver Brook like she does every Wednesday.

"You never elaborated on that text about Mr. Goldfarb the other day," she says. "Explain yourself."

"Okay, here goes. According to a reliable source, by which I mean me, your buddies the Goldfarbs have a nasty past. This is top secret from the CIA, or at least from Google. Mr. Goldfarb is Louie 'The Lung' Kleinfeld, son of a famous Jewish mafia kingpin. And his sweet, wrinkly wife is Bad News Bessie. They're notorious old-time gangsters on the run."

"Ooh, exactly what I suspected about that sweet couple moving three inches per hour with their walkers. ARE YOU NUTS?"

"Maybe, unless I'm right, in which case I'm brilliant."

"We need more to go on than that, Lewin."

"Agreed. I'm going to need your help to crack them."

We find our suspects watching TV in the dayroom. "Look, Sidney, here's the bar mitzvah boy and the bat mitzvah girl!" says Mrs. Goldfarb—or is it Kleinfeld?

Time to find out. "Hey, Tessa, remember Donald Duck?" I do my best *squawk-squawk* impersonation and waddle. "Remember how he was always ragging on his nephews—what were their names? Let's see, Huey and Dewey, but I can't pull up the third one."

Tessa has it: "Louie."

"*Louie*, oh yeah, Huey, Dewey, and LOUIE."

Not even a twitch of the cheek from Louie the Lung, who maybe isn't.

"Next are you gonna ask me the names of Cinderella's stepsisters?"

Great, Tessa's on board with my scheme! Looking all innocent and harmless: "I think one was named *Bessie*."

"Anastasia and Drizella," says Mrs. Goldfarb.

This is going nowhere, but I try one more time: "By the way, we won't be here next Wednesday because our b'nai mitzvah class is meeting with a class in Tulsa. That's *bad news*, isn't it?"

Bad News Bessie doesn't even twitch. Man, they're good, those Goldfarbs/Kleinfelds!

Mrs. Goldfarb says, "I hear you've met our Jeremy. Such a fine boy who loves his great-grandpa, doesn't he, Sidney? Jeremy, that's who we're talking about, silly man. The bar mitzvah boy is his little friend." She grins at me and points a bony hitchhike thumb as if to say *What am I gonna do with him?*

In my head I'm seeing Bad News Bessie sixty years younger, in skintight black, including a mask and leather gloves. She's jumping fences and bounding up fire escapes and scaling walls to score jewelry from the fourteenth floor of a Hoboken apartment building. And Louie the Lung is on the street, gunning the engine of the getaway car. True love, those two.

31

"My mother's pearls!" wails Mrs. Dorian right before dinnertime.

Tessa and I exchange looks as we rush over to her apartment, beating the rest of the residents by about an hour. Are the Goldfarbs behind this, with the plumber as their collaborator? But how do they manage the stairs to the basement? Unless their walkers are as bogus as Mr. Goldfarb's silence.

Ms. Brubaker comes running on those spiked heels, Flambé trotting at her side, and both of them clickety-clacking on the tile floor. "Surely you've just misplaced them, Rosa."

"Surely I have *not*. I keep them wrapped in pink tissue paper and a silk scarf that a student gave me forty years ago, tucked among the bloomers in my drawer. Well! The tissue and scarf are there, but my mother's pure perfect pearls are gone!"

Ms. Brubaker pivots and spots Tessa and me standing in the doorway. "Eddie, were you in Mrs. Dorian's room?"

"No, ma'am. I came like you did when I heard her yelling about her pearls."

Ms. Brubaker narrows her eyes. Officer Kinsey and Hank are there in a flash, like they've just been waiting around for this special moment in our lives.

"Officer, please take Eddie into my office. Hank, you go with. We're missing a string of pearls."

"My mother's pure, perfect pearls," Mrs. Dorian clarifies.

Flashing me a look of sympathy, Hank probably gets how spooked I am. He unlocks Ms. Brubaker's office, and once we're inside, the security guard butts the door shut.

Me, trying to sound tough, while my heart's hammering: "My parents have to be here. It's the law."

Kinsey, unimpressed: "You an expert on Oklahoma law? Empty every pocket, then turn each one inside out." Done. "Shoes and socks off." He pokes around in the shoes and shakes the overripe socks, sniffing them Flambé-style. Man, what a way to make a living.

He could be gentler patting me down, especially in the tender area. He even scratches around in my mop of hair. Yeah, I need a haircut, so there's enough of it that I could harbor a nest of spiders, but he seems satisfied that no pearls are hiding on my head or in my ears or up my nose, where he shines a pen-point flashlight. Can I sue him for this?

Hank says, "I believe the boy's clean."

"Mebbe, mebbe not."

Ms. Brubaker joins us as I'm pulling my socks back on, hopping on one foot. I sling my backpack over one shoulder. "Are we done here, sir?" I ask.

Kinsey's eyes narrow. "The backpack. Drop it."

Flambé scurries out of the way when my backpack clonks to the floor. Fake-Cop Kinsey keeps one eye on me as he lifts and unzips it. Out come my math book, my baseball mitt and batting glove, wads of crumpled paper, six stubby pencils, a couple of empty Snickers wrappers, my homework agenda. Other stuff. Nothing embarrassing like a jock cup.

"Typical kid's mess," Hank says with a nervous chuckle.

"Mm-hmm." Officer Kinsey turns the backpack upside down and dumps out crumbs that have been on the bottom since sixth grade, an empty Pez container and . . . and . . . a gold ring that jangles onto the table!

No. How did that get in there? My face stings.

Hank sinks into the scratchy chair. The look on his face says he's disappointed in me.

"It's not . . . I didn't . . . I don't know how . . ." Am I making sense? Am I digging my own grave?

Like on TV, Kinsey takes out a handkerchief and lifts the ring, holds it up to the light to read whatever it says inside. *To Thelma. Love, Enoch.*

"Thelma?" Kinsey asks, and Ms. Brubaker fills in the blank: "Mrs. Boniface."

"Can you explain this, son?" He's throwing me a lifeline, but I can't explain why Thelma Boniface's stolen ring is in my backpack.

Ms. Brubaker shakes her head sadly. "She trusted you, Eddie. I don't want to press charges, but you *must* return every item you've stolen immediately. If you don't, it'll be out of my hands and in the hands of the authorities."

"How can I return things I never took?" I shout.

Kinsey slits his eyes until they laser into me. "Edward Lewin—"

My heart drops like a marble on cement. He'll say *Edward Lewin, you're under arrest,* and then he'll

Miranda me, read me my rights to remain silent and to get a lawyer. He'll tell me anything I say can and will be used against me in a court of law. I whoosh in my breath and try not to squirm while marbles pinball against the walls of my chest.

"I'm recommending to Ms. Brubaker that you take a leave of absence."

I'm so scared I can barely rasp the words out. "What's that mean?"

"It means your whatsamacallit mitzvoo project is over. You're outta here. If I have to get a court order, you betcha I will. Get your shoes and socks on, son, and head right for the nearest exit. Do not pass Go, do not collect two hundred dollars. Vamoose."

"But—"

"That's enough." Ms. Brubaker points to the gold ring on the desk and says, "You've given me no choice, Eddie. You are not to set foot in Silver Brook from here on out, understand?"

"You'll be hearing from us," Officer Kinsey adds threateningly, waving me out of his sight.

I am in deep, deep trouble.

32

I've gotta tell Mom and Dad that I've been kicked out of Silver Brook. But the bills spread across the kitchen table shout *NOT NOW*. Dad chews on an eraser as Mom waves a stack in each hand. "These we can put aside. No penalty for late payment. Oh, hi, Eddie. But these we have to pay immediately."

Dad's been applying for jobs over half the state of Oklahoma, but nobody is hiring a produce manager. Don't they realize how important our recommended daily allowance of fruits and veggies is?

And now, to add to the rest of the family grief, I'm a suspected criminal.

"Don't worry about the power company cutting off our electricity," Gabby assures us. "I'll rig up a system so we'll get juice off the grid."

"They're not cutting off our electricity!" Mom cries.

I gotta tell them, gotta tell them.

Dad tosses a pencil across the room. "Maybe I should go back to school, get an MBA that'll land me a top management position instead of the small-potatoes fruits and vegetables."

"Where would we get the money for tuition, Jake? Especially without your income," Mom points out. "I'm already doing my editing work more than full time." She looks over at me again. "Eddie? Isn't this a Silver Brook day?"

"It was." I sink down into an empty chair at the table. "We gotta talk. Gabby, this is between me and Mom and Dad, so, uh . . ."

"I can take a hint." She stomps out of the room.

My face hangs heavy in my hands, elbows puckering the padded tablecloth.

Dad stabs another pencil into a thick stack of papers. "What's going on, Eddie?"

My eyes are leaking and I can hardly breathe.

Mom rushes to grab a tissue for me, then sits back down and wraps her arms around my shoulders. "What is it, honey?"

Between gasps: "Mrs. Boniface . . . the one we're

doing the robot for . . . the thief stole her wedding ring."

"I know you're very fond of her, honey."

"You don't understand! They found her wedding ring in the bottom of my backpack!"

Dad rears back so far that he nearly topples his chair. "How did it get there, Eddie?"

"I don't know! I didn't steal it!"

Gabby, of course, has been listening from the living room. "Obviously, somebody planted it in Eddie's backpack to frame him."

"You might as well come in," Dad calls to Gabby. "But who would do something like that?"

"I don't know!" I yell again, all nasally.

Dad jumps up. "We'll go right over there and have a chat with that rude rent-a-cop."

Mom shakes her head. Her face is feverish-red. "No, Jake. We have to find a lawyer right now before this goes any further. Eddie, there's one of those jumbo pickles you love in the fridge, and Gabby, I think you have a book report due tomorrow."

This means *Get out of here so we can talk about you.*

The pickle's so cold that my front teeth ache all the way up the bridge of my nose. One bite and I

realize that it's just as sour as I feel. Except I'm scared
to death. The pickle's a lot braver.

My phone pings with a text.

Tessa: I'm at SB. Boss is in an uproar!

Me: Over me?

Tessa: Over, under, all around.

Me: Anyone miss me yet?

**Tessa: There's weeping and wailing, esp.
Mrs. Boniface. Well, not wailing.**

Me: What's going on with the spy cam?

**Tessa: Who knows? Haven't been able to
detour to the basement. If her eyeballs aren't
locked on to me, she's got poor Hank on
the job.**

Me: Probably thinks we're in cahoots.

(Long pause, which confirms it.)

Me: Meeting with a lawyer soon.

Tessa: Gulp.

The lawyer Dad's found is Mr. Palmer, a Black retired
army sergeant who's now a third-year law school student volunteering at the legal aid clinic. Mom and
Dad make me wear khakis and a button-down shirt

and real shoes, but it turns out that the lawyer is in jeans and a T-shirt and retro Air Jordans.

"See?" I hiss at my parents.

"This is serious," Dad hisses back.

I pour the story out to Mr. Palmer. "I'm not the thief, sir."

"And the ring in your backpack, Mr. Lewin?"

Dad starts to answer, then realizes the lawyer is calling *me* Mr. Lewin. Should I call him Sergeant Palmer?

"I guess my parents told you about that."

He tents his fingers and waits.

"My best guess is that someone stashed it there as evidence against me. The ring belongs to my favorite resident at Silver Brook. Why would I take something that's important to her?"

Mr. Palmer sizes me up. He never blinks. "I believe you, Mr. Lewin. But please understand that there's clear evidence against you, and it's your word against everyone else's."

"He's innocent," Mom says calmly, locking Dad's arm in place.

"Understood. Still, this could get unpleasant before your son is cleared of all accusations. Have you told me everything, Mr. Lewin?"

"Everything, yeah." Except I don't tell him that I've been doing my own investigation, or about the Goldfarbs and the mob. I need to do more research before I point the finger at them.

Mr. Palmer reminds us that he's on my side, but the way he talks makes me want to stand at attention and say *sir yes sir*. "Two things, Mr. Lewin. You do not speak to anyone about this without me at your side— and that includes the administrator at Silver Brook, the police, or the facility's lawyer. Second, you do not step foot inside that place until I tell you all clear, got that?"

"Yes, sir."

"Fine. Parents, I'll get right to work on this. We will keep your son out of juvenile detention."

Back home, I can't wait to ditch these starchy clothes. The knees don't even bend.

Before dashing off to another hopeless job interview, Dad says, "Let's think about postponing the bar mitzvah."

Postpone it? Big relief. Or is it? I'd be letting my whole family down. Not just my family; Rabbi Kefler and thousands of years of history that's like a trail behind me—which reminds me of Dad saying I've got a responsibility to make sure history doesn't twist the way it did during World War II.

Ms. Brubaker and Fake-Cop Kinsey are satisfied they've found their thief, so it's up to me to catch the real crooks.

The plumber, Matt Bowers, must be involved. And as for his partners—we have genuine, professional underworld mobsters living right there in Silver Brook. It's gotta be the Goldfarbs. They fit the job description, with the means, motive, and opportunity. But how can I prove it if I can't even set foot inside the building?

There's Got. To. Be. A. Way.

33

All my life Mom's song has been, "Look at the bright side, Eddie," as in, "Yes, you slammed the car door on your finger, but look at the bright side. It could have been your whole hand, or your tongue."

What's the bright side now? I'm the only suspect, and it's not just small stuff that's missing. It's Mrs. Callahan's watch, Maurie's diamond tie pin, Mr. Archer's ten big ones, Mrs. Dorian's pearls.

And Thelma Boniface's ring in my backpack.

Word gets around. People who don't know the first thing about Silver Brook look away when our eyes meet. I hear them thinking, *Did he do it? Is he a low-down sniveling crook who steals from innocent seniors?*

I admit it: I'm scared, but also bored. Sure, I'm busy with Robotics Club and Zippy, with Rabbi Kefler's class, and, oh yeah, school. But, believe it or not, I'm homesick for Silver Brook. What if one of the old folks passes away, and I'm not there? What if Lina misses picking on me? What if Thelma Boniface thinks I've forgotten about her or, worse, thinks I stole her ring? I can't even get back to Silver Brook to tell her I didn't do it!

And I'm running out of time to log my hours there, which means I can kiss my bar mitzvah goodbye, especially if I end up in juvie.

But, yeah, Mom, I have to look at the bright side, which is . . . which is . . . that I have Monday and Wednesday afternoons free. More time to shovel up dirt on Louie the Lung and Bad News Bessie while the lawyer does his thing and I wait for my doom.

＝＝＝

Amazing what you find on the internet. Louie the Lung hasn't paid taxes in eleven years. The white George Washington hair on his head started off on someone else's, I guess, since Louie got hair plug transplants in 2012. And the biggest revelation? He has only one kidney, because a bullet exploded in the other one, in mob crossfire. To find out for sure whether Mr. Goldfarb is Louie the Lung, I have to know how many kidneys he has stowed away in his lumpy body.

Easier said than done. I can't show my face at Silver Brook to ask questions or push the guy under an X-ray machine.

While I'm chewing on this problem, I keep researching. The internet is loaded with websites on gangster stuff, and I'm having a feast. Too bad I don't spend as much time on Spanish or Hebrew vocab as I've been spending on gangster-speak. Jeez, I could write a story. In fact, one is streaming in my mind right now.

King Charles Solomon, the Russian Jewish mob boss in Boston, and Louie the Lung from Hoboken are sitting on overturned paint drums (Ecru Enamel and Skylight Semi-Gloss) in some dark alley. Both are packing heat. The Boss says, "Your doll Bessie, she ain't cracked a safe or broke a knee in three months. I need some action, Louie, or you're both gonna be sleepin' wid de fishes."

Wait, I think I got that from an old Godfather movie.

"It shoulda been duck soup, Louie, but you and Bessie, you're A1 lousy thieves."

Would it be worse to be accused of being a thief (*I'm no thief!* I keep shouting to myself) or worse to be a failure as a thief? Well, anyway, I'm a chicken. I'd have been no good in the mob.

Mom interrupts the movie playing in my head. "Eddie, I asked you to take the blue bin out to the road. Look at the bright side, honey. It could be stinky garbage instead of recycling."

Back to normal life, sort of.

34

While our pitcher and catcher are huddling with Coach on the mound, I've got one eye on the Edmond runner trying to lead off here at first, and the other on a stranger in a trench coat, standing a couple feet behind the ump. He steps back when the ump yells, "Play ball," and the next batter comes to the plate.

Man, we should have expected the sacrifice bunt down the third-base line. Batter's out, but the two runners advance, safe at second and third, and here comes Edmond's powerhouse hitter. Doom.

One of the guys in their dugout yells, "Hey, Lewin, let 'im *steal* a base!"

"Yeah," another guy says, "watch the runner on third. He could be *caught stealing home.*"

I square my shoulders and turn my back, but it stings.

The next pitch is high and outside, the batter swings and misses, and the ump yells, "You're out!" Like it was planned, the whole Edmond dugout stands up and shouts, "He was *robbed*!"

Sheesh, does the entire state know I'm an accused thief? Is it breaking news? My teeth are clenched, my face is hot. Wish I could punch something, anything.

Coach walks over with Jordy Bennet. "Lewin, I'm putting Bennet in. Have a seat and cool off, son."

In our dugout, I slam my glove so hard that it bounces and raises a cloud of dry Oklahoma dirt. Nobody says a word.

After the game, the trench coat guy hooks his finger to call me over. Gabby and Mom stand behind me, a hand on each of my shoulders. "Great catch at first, Eddie," the guy says, like we're pals.

"Who are you?" Mom asks.

He pats around his coat pocket and pulls out an ID. "Detective Apodaca, Oklahoma City Police Department, ma'am. Eddie, let's talk."

"I didn't do it!"

Mom grabs her phone out of her purse. "I'm calling our lawyer."

"No need, ma'am. It's a friendly chat." Oh man, he's here to arrest me. Well, I don't see handcuffs hanging out of his pocket, but whatever happens, it's not gonna be a winning run for me.

"Mr. Palmer?" Mom says into the phone. "We're at Greenmeadow Park with Detective Apodaca," Mom says. "What should we do? Sure. We'll wait right here."

Mom won't let Detective Apodaca say a word to me until both teams are gone and Mr. Palmer pulls into the parking lot—on a Harley. He takes off his helmet, grabs his briefcase off the back of the bike, says, "ID?" and nods when the detective flashes it.

The five of us sit in the bleachers, Gabby squeezing my hand. Times like this Gabby acts like a real kid, same as me, and believe me, I'm scared so bad that my toenails are rattling loose in my socks.

"So, Detective, what brings you here this evening?" demands Mr. Palmer.

"Let's everybody chill." The detective pulls out his notebook and a pen. "You okay, Eddie?"

"Yes, sir." If *okay* includes my gut turning trampoline backflips.

"Your case landed on my to-do pile today. I did some checking at Silver Brook. Call me curious, but what makes you so popular with the residents?"

Mr. Palmer's nodding, encouraging me to answer, but his eyebrows are raised in a *be careful* signal.

"I listen to their stories."

"Unusual for a young teen to be so patient with oldsters."

"Seniors, sir. That's the proper designation."

Mr. Palmer says, "Get to the point, Detective."

"Eddie, in your own words, what's the scene at Silver Brook? I hear valuables have gone missing."

"I'll allow him to answer," Mr. Palmer says, "but I'll stop him and consult with my client whenever I see fit."

"Expected," the detective says neutrally.

"I started at Silver Brook a couple months ago," I begin. "My mom made me." Out of the corner of my eye I see her smile. "Turned out to be a good thing because those seniors are pretty cool. Two of the men are always in a fight, but they really like each other. One lady, she had a stroke before I got to Silver Brook, so she can only use one side of her body, and she's sad all the time, because nobody comes to visit her. I cheer her up." Suddenly, my thoughts about so many of them pour out—Mrs. Callahan with the fruit hats and cigar holder and the heroic past; Mrs. DiAngelo, the purple lady; cranky Lina, who's survived so much tragedy and loves baseball and used to sing in a nightclub; Earl Archer, head over heels in love with a woman who's practically older than the state of Oklahoma.

"Any of those folks lose valuables?"

"Most of 'em, sir. I didn't take any of their stuff, I swear it."

Gabby adds, "He's a pain in the neck as a brother, but he's no thief."

The detective's smile is almost reassuring. "So, who stole those things, Eddie?"

"I don't know. But I have two suspects. I have reason to believe that two members of the mob are living at Silver Brook."

"The mob, uh-huh." He seems disappointingly calm, when I was hoping he'd leap up and say, *Organized crime? Lead me to them!*

My voice kind of wobbles until I get going. "Yes, sir. This old couple at Silver Brook, Sydney and Ruth Goldfarb? Their real name is Kleinfeld. They're wanted! They've been on the run since around 1960."

Detective Apodaca doesn't write anything in his notebook.

"Um, Eddie," says Mom, "are you sure . . ."

"Mom, I've done *research*! Louie the Lung only has one kidney, so Detective, if you're in doubt, find out how many kidneys Mr. Goldfarb has."

"Uh-huh," Detective Apodaca says again. "And let's say these folks do have a criminal past. What's it got to do with you, Eddie?"

"Isn't it obvious?" I fight the urge to stomp my foot. "I mean, sir, if stuff's been stolen at Silver Brook, and two known burglars live there, why would you need any other suspects? Me, for instance."

"Mr. Lewin," says my lawyer sharply, "I'd advise you not to say more about this right now."

The detective flips his notebook shut. "I'll look into it, Eddie. If it turns out you're right about these folks, it's a matter for the FBI. I'll have some more questions for you after I investigate further."

"My son's on a deadline, Detective," Mom jumps in. "His volunteer work at Silver Brook is required for a major milestone event in June."

Detective Apodaca smiles. "Noted, Mrs. Lewin. I'll see what I can do."

Days pass without a word from Detective Apodaca or my lawyer. At least nobody's come with handcuffs or a search warrant for under my bed, where things living and dead could be happily sharing real estate.

"What's taking the police so long with the Goldfarbs?" I demand over the weekend.

"The wheels of justice grind slowly," Dad says—one of his cornier lines. He's pretty distracted because he has a big phone interview coming up. "I imagine the FBI would have to build a solid case against them before taking them into custody. Focus on something else, Eddie, such as YOUR BAR MITZVAH SPEECH?"

Considering that my bar mitzvah may or may not be happening, I haven't felt especially inspired to write the speech.

"The 'wheels of justice' thing, that would make an awesome opening line," Gabby says. "Want me to write your speech for you?"

"Would you? I'll give you my fourth most valuable baseball card, which is a 1992 Nolan Ryan."

"That doesn't impress me. I've already got two weeks of your allowance."

"Something I should know?" Dad asks, and we both flash our most angelic expressions.

···

The kidney thing, that would prove that Mr. Goldfarb and Louie the Lung are the same guy. Wish I could sneak into Ms. Brubaker's office and find his medical records. How hard could that be . . . for a kid who can't set foot in the place?

Besides, Ms. Brubaker always locks her office with the key she wears around her neck.

But Hank! He has keys to everything. I can ask him for help!

35

I look up the main number for Silver Brook and key it into my phone. If I really work at it, I can disguise my voice into something like a baritone, but the person on the other end has to have crummy hearing.

Judy answers: "Silver Brook Pavilion. How may I help you?"

"Uh, yes, would you be so kind as to connect me with Hank Fridell?"

"Who shall I say is calling, sweetie?"

"Um, his son, one of them." He's gotta have at least two.

"Hold on a sec, sweetie." Judy bellows over the intercom, which could wake up the near-dead at Silver Brook, "Hank, phone call, sweetie." I guess I'm not the only sweetie in her life. The list probably also includes Fake-Cop Kinsey, who's always hanging over her desk, except when he's terrorizing me.

Hank's voice in my ear: "Yes?"

"Hank, it's me, Eddie."

"You doing okay, man? Kinsey was kind of harsh with you." He doesn't mention the ring or his disappointment.

"I need a huge, humongous favor. Can you get into Ms. Brubaker's office and check some medical files for me?"

"You asking me to do this without Ms. Brubaker knowing it?"

"Well, kind of."

"Kind of, or *all* of?"

I hear the suspicion in Hank's voice. He knows a con when he hears one.

"Look, I'm zeroing in on who the real thief is. You know it's not me, don't you?"

He doesn't say anything, and my heart drops.

"Okay, I know it sounds weird, but I have to find out how many kidneys a certain resident has."

"The standard number is two, Eddie. You don't have to take my math class to figure that out."

"That's just the thing. This person has one."

"Why are you needing to know about anybody's kidneys?"

"Can't tell you yet. Please? It's super important."

"I'm in deep hot water, I'm talking *boiling*, if anybody finds out I've been conspiring with you, much less violating residents' privacy. It's my job on the line, man."

"I know, and I'd owe you forever, but this could affect everyone at Silver Brook," I plead.

No answer for a few seconds, and I get my hopes up. Finally: "After thinking a minute, no. I won't sneak into the office and paw around in confidential files."

I swallow dry spit. "Okay, then what if I got into the office on my own? Where would I find everybody's medical history?"

"Not my department. Besides, you're not supposed to show your face here, Eddie."

I sigh. "I just want to help fix this."

There's dead air again for way too long, until Hank says, "Even if you got into the office, that spoiled-rotten dog wouldn't let you near anything. Ever see all those pictures, Flambé's whole family of show-offs standing there like the kings and queens of England? I don't know about you, but my heart goes out to that poor relative who hides his head in shame. That's the one I'd take home to my babies, if I could."

"Yeah," I whisper, defeated. Until it hits me: he's just told me which cabinet the medical records are in! "Thanks, Hank. By the way, how's everybody doing at Silver Brook?"

"Mrs. DiAngelo misses your sweet, purple face. Lina is missing you too, in her own way. These seniors get under your skin, don't they? God love 'em." Pause. "Be careful, Eddie. Don't jump into water over your head. Could be sharks."

Such as Hester Brubaker. He doesn't like her any better than I do.

36

I'm getting a call from an unknown number. I answer it, thinking maybe it's Hank calling me back on his cell. Instead, I hear Earl Archer's voice.

"Hello? Is this thing on?"

"Hey, Mr. Archer! Yeah, it's working. I can hear you."

"Eddie! I got your number from Tessa. Wanted to see how you were holding up."

"I'm okay. What about you? What's new at Silver Brook? Has anything else disappeared since I left?"

"Nope. Doesn't look good for you, sonny, I gotta say."

"But I'm not the thief, Mr. Archer! You believe me, don't you?"

"Sure I do. But the real thief's doing a top-notch job of framing you. Which means you're gonna miss the most exciting night of the year here—the annual spring sleepover on Saturday night. All the grandkids and great-grandkids bring their sleeping bags and spend the night in the dayroom. Tessa's gonna be here the whole time. Wish you could do the same, sonny."

Light bulb over my head!

"Same, Mr. Archer. Hey, has Mrs. Perlmuter accepted your proposal yet?"

"Still holding out for someone younger and richer. But I haven't given up hope!"

※ ※ ※

"Why *can't* we ask Mr. Palmer if I can go back to Silver Brook?"

"Eddie, you know why."

"Just for Saturday night, Mom? It's the spring sleepover, the seniors' favorite thing in the whole year." At least according to Earl Archer.

Though she's shaking her head, Mom gets Mr. Palmer on speaker phone. "Not possible, Mr. Lewin. You're by no means free and clear, not until I hear from Detective Apodaca that you're no longer a person of interest. As the saying goes, it ain't over till it's over."

I have to respect him for quoting Yogi Berra, though my language arts teacher would have a fit if she heard the grammar. "But sir, the seniors need me. Mrs. Boniface is counting on my company, and counting on my robotics squad to bring back her interactive friend, Zippy. Lina Kempinski, well, she's nuts about baseball, and I'm the only baseball player in her life . . ."

"I hear you're getting phone calls from one of the residents, Mr. Earl Archer."

How does he know?

"From where the Silver Brook administrator sits, it could look like you're collaborating with someone on the inside. Now, you don't want to implicate that fine old gentleman. My advice? Watch your step. No more phone chats with Mr. Archer, hear?"

Sir yes sir. Hanging up, I whine to Mom, even though whining is off-limits in the Lewin house. "How am I going to finish my mitzvah project hours?"

"Maybe Rabbi Kefler will make an exception," Mom says unconvincingly. A split second later, though, she hits me with this: "My parents canceled their flights just in case."

"Hey!" If you can't count on your grandparents to believe in you, who can you count on?

A good old, one-hundred-percent reliable, rolling bucket of squeaks and squeals, that's who. I've been logging a lot of time working on Zippy after school, even when Azmara and Joe aren't there. I know it's weird, but I've told Zippy all about the mess I'm in, even stuff the lawyer doesn't know.

Zippy's good at keeping secrets. But she's not much of a detective.

I've got to get back to Silver Brook.

And I need a co-conspirator.

Lockers slam all around us. Chopsticks poke out of Tessa's bushy hair like horns. She sees me looking at the neon-pink stripe of hair circling her face. "This? Yeah, my mom hates it worse than the blue. She'll disown me if the pink's not grown out by my bat mitzvah."

"Hey, Tessa, you know how to pick locks?"

"Why? Is your Hello Kitty diary jammed?"

"I mean real locks."

"Safecracking isn't one of my skill sets." Her locker is jam-packed, but she crams in a puffy vest and slams the door to prevent an avalanche. "Okay,

Lewin, what's on your warped mind?"

"I need you to help me prove that Mr. Goldfarb has only one kidney."

"Like I've got X-ray vision to see through his baggy sweats?" She shifts her skull-and-crossbones backpack and tucks a wisp of cotton-candy hair behind her ear. "Oh, sure, I'll announce, 'Everybody in the room with two kidneys, raise your hand.' Or how about this: 'Mrs. Goldfarb, is your husband missing anything, like a hairbrush or a shoehorn or, um, I dunno, a *kidney?*'"

"There's a way."

"Send your robot to get the info?" She stops suddenly, and I stumble into her. "Wait, you're not suggesting I hack into Madame Brubaker's computer and read Mr. Goldfarb's medical information, are you?"

"No! Give me more credit than that."

"What a relief."

"I'm suggesting you sneak into her office and steal the physical copy of his medical information."

"How is that better?!"

"There's no hacking involved? And I've . . . got a hunch that I know where those files are."

"A hunch?"

"Yup." I'm not gonna drag Hank into this.

"Then do it yourself! Oh, right. Poor Eddie's been banished from paradise."

If she were anybody but Tessa—like the whole Edmond baseball team, for instance—she'd be thinking, *If you can steal a ring from poor Mrs. Boniface, stealing medical records is a piece of cake.*

After a deep sigh, Tessa says, "Okay, I'm in. You know why? Because well-behaved women seldom make history. I'm going for the history books."

"Awesome. So, here's the diabolical plan. This Saturday night when all the grandkids and great-grandkids are there with sleeping bags, you'll be there, right? So . . ." After checking around for spying ears, I whisper the rest. Her eyes zoom wide, but she doesn't say no.

37

Gabby's covering for me at home, but there's a price. I pledge her the rest of my allowance until my bar mitzvah. "And if there's no bar mitzvah," she says, "I get half your allowance until you go to college." If Mom and Dad find out what I'm up to, I'll be grounded until I'm seventy-two and won't need allowance anyway.

No lights splash the side door of the Silver Brook building, not even a glimmer of moonlight. My backpack thumps against me as I hold my nose and crouch between the stinky black garbage bags.

The door swings open just enough to let me squeeze through. Tessa's on all fours, on the floor. "Stay under the motion detectors," she whispers. We both crawl down the hall until we're clear of the sensors she's scouted out.

"Do you realize how much grief I'll get if Madame Brubaker finds out I let you in? You owe me big time, Lewin!"

"I know! You're the best." Yikes, did I say that out loud?

Tessa pulls me into the one-iMac lab. "Brubaker's still in her office, but she gave a little welcome speech earlier and she'll be back soon to do the goodnight speech. That's when we make our move."

From where we're hiding, we can hear someone strumming a guitar in the dayroom.

"That's Mrs. Callahan's granddaughter, Sheree," Tessa explains, as the song leader shouts, "Is everybody ready?! Come on, every one of you, sing your hearts out! Raise some heat! Feel the beat!" She strums, and they sing until the chandelier must be swaying.

"Ms. Brubaker isn't staying here all night, is she?" I whisper to Tessa. "Can't we wait to search her office until she leaves?"

Tessa shakes her head. "Connie, the night nurse, told me that Brubaker always sticks around on the night of the sleepover. Dozes at her desk till morning, just in case there's an incident with the kids' behavior. Our one shot at the office will be when she announces that it's time for the seniors to head back to their apartments and time for the kids to settle down in the dayroom."

This is just my luck. What seemed like the perfect chance to get access to Ms. Brubaker's office is actually a narrow window of opportunity.

We peek into the dayroom as Lina's old boyfriend from Paris, Mr. Caliberti, bursts onto the scene and grabs a mic. "Members of Canto's Chorus, weave your way up here. Show our audience what we've been practicing every Tuesday morning!"

Ten people struggle out of their chairs or swing their wheelchairs and walkers around to cluster in front of Mr. Caliberti, who elbows his way to the front again and addresses the audience with lots of flair. "Ladies and gentlemen, we present our signature number." He spins around dramatically to face his chorus, raises his hands, and snaps his fingers in the air. "A one and a two and a . . ."

"*There's NO business like SHOW business*," they belt out to wild applause from whoever's still awake. The grandkids get everybody off their tushes to dance, like it's a bar mitzvah party. Right on cue, Sheree slides into "Hava Nagila," and Mrs. Perlmuter grabs Earl Archer and grapevines him around the room. He lights up like a firecracker when she plants a smackeroo on his stubbly cheek. Man, I've missed these crusty old seniors!

That's when we hear Ms. Brubaker's heels—followed by Flambé's paws—clicking down the hallway and toward the dayroom. Tessa yanks my arm. "Okay, this is it! Showtime!"

38

Step one: get into Hester Brubaker's locked office. I thought about this a lot ahead of time. I figured the famous plastic credit card trick might work, but, hey, I'm thirteen—no credit card. So instead, I've stashed an ice pick in my backpack. Between that and Mrs. Boniface's ring, this backpack is turning into a pretty impressive trove of incriminating evidence.

I nearly impale myself rummaging blindly through my bag in the dark, but out comes the ice pick, which I stab into the keyhole a few dozen times. Payday! It catches on something, and we hear the beautiful music of the latch turning. We're in! But we don't dare turn on the lights.

"Are we great burglars, or are we great burglars?" Tessa boasts.

"Hey, I'm the one who thought to bring the

ice pick. Those cabinets under the bookshelves, I'm pretty sure the medical files are in there."

"The doors with the dog pictures on them?" Tessa hunches over her phone so the light won't show under the office door. "This cabinet? With the pitiful black sheep of Flambé's world-famous family?"

"Feels right."

"Too small for file folders . . . unless they're digitized records, maybe on an iPad."

The trusty ice pick goes to work like it's on a mission with a criminal mind of its own. The lock is the little round kind flat against the cabinet, but when you hit it right, the lock pops out—*sprong!*—like one of those paper snakes in a can.

"Yes!"

"Shh!" Tessa warns.

Inside is one deep drawer that might have held physical files in its previous life. Now about a hundred little thumb drives rattle around on the bottom. Tessa dumps handfuls onto the carpet, which soaks up the sound, and I grab the phone away from her to wash its light over the tangle of flash drives.

No names on them, just numbers. After each number there's a letter: 213B, 136E. "All of 'em have three digits and an alpha-letter."

"Letter for the last name?" Tessa ventures.

"Good a guess as any."

"Maybe we should be looking for a master list by number."

"Hey, Tessa, we can read English *and* Hebrew. How hard can it be for us to crack this code?"

Pretty hard. All the flash drives dumped on the floor make a small mountain of digital mishmash.

"Face it, Eddie. These are random old thumb drives. They could be, like, all of Brubaker's college notes, or every third-rate poem she ever wrote, or . . ."

"Or records for every resident at Silver Brook."

"Hear that? Someone's out there." We both slam down on the floor like flatworms.

A toilet flushes across the hall and we hear footsteps disappearing toward the dayroom, where they're drowned out by a bone-chilling scream and the creepy *Friday the Thirteenth* music.

"We're missing a good movie," Tessa says. "Like I said, you owe me. Okay, let's turn all the thumb drives over and look for a *G*."

There are seven Gs. "We can't take them all," Tessa says.

Defeated by something the size of my thumb?

No way. "We could stick each of them into the desktop and see what pops up."

"Seriously? It could take all night, and the screen light would blow our cover. Any other ideas?"

"I'm thinking. Can't you hear the ticking in my brain?"

"Just heavy breathing. You're starting to panic, Lewin."

"Am not. Okay, here's a theory. The numbers represent the first three or last three digits of their social security number."

"Which we don't know," Tessa mutters. "Hey, look. On each of them, the first digit is a one, two, three, or four. Nothing higher than four."

"Four seasons? Four-leaf clover? The Four Questions from Passover?"

"The four humors: blood, phlegm, yellow bile, and black bile?" Tessa adds.

"Forget bile." With a sweeping gesture to his family portraits, I say, "Flambé has four legs."

"So do an elephant and a table. Your point?"

Hmm . . . "How many years has Silver Brook been here? Could it be *four* years?"

"Could be. So you're saying the first digit represents the year the resident arrived. What if the next two numbers are the order they came to Silver Brook?"

"Yeah, then the biggest number would be the most recent comer, ya think?"

"Makes sense."

"And the Goldfarbs have only lived here about three months. Find the highest numbered 4-blank-blank-G."

Tessa's phone light hovers over our hoard on the floor. "Here it is: 422G. We've got it, Lewin, because here's 421G. Mister and Missus!"

"But which is which?"

Tessa turns the two thumb drives over in her palm. "There's a weird little symbol drawn on the label. This one has a tiny arrow pointing up to the right side, and the other's got a cross pointing down from the center. Religious symbols? I get the cross, but what about the arrow? Madame Brubaker could be discriminating on the basis of religion!"

"Relax," I say, "I know what the icons are. It's like matching electronic parts for a robot, so 421G with the arrow is male and 422G is female."

She snatches the female out of my hand and kisses it. "Ruthie Goldfarb, you are my woman!"

"Quiet, somebody's coming! Hit the floor!"

39

I slip Mr. Goldfarb into my hoodie pocket as we scramble under the desk.

The door opens. Ms. Brubaker says, "That's odd. I'm sure I locked the door, with all these unruly monster children here. Did you unlock it, Connie?"

"No, ma'am, I was supervising the young guests in the dayroom until you called me away."

They burst into the office, and suddenly I remember the dozens of thumb drives scattered over the floor, and the open cabinet door. Which Ms. Brubaker now spots.

"Good Lord! We've been robbed!" She pushes the night nurse out of the office, slamming the door behind them, and we hear them running down the hall.

We scurry out of there and head for the side door so I can make my escape. *Friday the Thirteenth* is still blasting from the dayroom. All the residents are tucked away in their apartments, and the grandkids are bingeing on junk food and horror. Sounds good to me, but I can't afford to stick around.

Behind us, we hear the *clump clump* of a walker, and walkers don't have their own legs.

We swivel around.

"Who's there?" Mrs. 422G's voice is a growl, fierce and hoarse, as if she just woke up. Or is it because somebody caught her on her middle-of-the-night thievery rounds? But when she recognizes Tessa, she switches to her super-sweet voice. "Why, it's the bat mitzvah girl. Who's that behind you?"

No choice but to slide out into view.

Mrs. 422G squints. "The bar mitzvah boy? I thought you weren't allowed here."

Tessa says, "It's three a.m. What are you doing up, Mrs. Goldfarb?"

"I'm looking for my Jeremy. Do you know where he is?"

"Asleep in the dayroom," I offer.

"Oh, of course! And you two?"

Just when I say, "Checking to make sure Ms. Brubaker's door is locked," Tessa murmurs, "She sent us to get her toothbrush."

Oh, yeah, who *wouldn't* believe us?

"My sweet Sidney was snoring so robustly that I couldn't sleep. He got up to tinkle, and I simply couldn't find my way to dreamland."

Tessa and I are thinking the same thing, but only she has the nerve to ask: "Does he have weak *kidneys*?" drawing out the final *s*, as in *not one*.

"Most certainly, in our advanced years. At your age you're like camels, but just you wait. I'm going to stop in the kitchen to see if there's a smidge of leftover chicken fricassee. Mm–*mmm*, it was tasty!"

Tessa and I wait until Mrs. 422G clumps out of sight. "Kitchen? Hah!" I mutter. "Bet she was on her way to steal something else. Bet she ditches her walker when she sneaks into someone's room. Bad News Bessie on a mission. Gotta hope she doesn't tell Ms. Brubaker she saw me."

We tiptoe the rest of the way down the hall and shove the side door open a second before Tessa's flashlight shines on a warning. "Oh, no, I forgot!"

OPENING THIS DOOR AFTER MIDNIGHT
SETS OFF A SECURITY ALARM.

Woo-OOP, Woo-OOP, Woo-OOP, Woo-OOP, the

alarm screeches and wails, and half the population of Oklahoma City comes running, led by Ms. Brubaker.

"Everyone stay calm," she says when she spots us. "Connie, kill the alarm, please. I'll handle these two." The crowd scatters, lurking in doorways to get the scoop.

Ms. Brubaker lets loose. "Eddie Lewin! How did you get into the building?"

Tessa takes a stab at a cover story: "Mrs. Goldfarb was up in the middle of the night, and . . ."

"You want to blame this on dear Mrs. Goldfarb? I'm supposed to believe *she* let Eddie in? No, Tessa, you did it, tell me the truth."

There's something unusual in Tessa's eyes. Fear. She links her little finger in mine. At least we're swimming in this shark-infested water together.

I try to save her from drowning. "Sorry, Ms. Brubaker. I knew this was the night of the sleepover, and I just didn't want to miss the fun." Feeble.

"Did the *fun* include ransacking my office?" Ms. Brubaker smooths her rumpled shirt. "Do you realize, Eddie, that I could have you arrested for breaking and entering?"

That chills my blood, until Tessa says, "Oh, Ms. Brubaker, if you only knew what we know."

40

After yanking us back into her office, Ms. Brubaker slams and locks the door. We're trapped! "Now then, what do you *think* you know?" she asks in a voice chilly enough to harden ice cream. I sneak a look at the pile of flash drives with a stab of guilt. My lawyer will kill me, if my parents don't do it first.

I take a deep breath. "We have it on authority, from an unnamed source, under a pledge of anonymity, that Mr. and Mrs. Goldfarb have a history of—"

"They're connected to the mob!" Tessa bursts out.

"For heaven's sake," scoffs Ms. Brubaker, plopping into her office chair so hard that papers on her desk take flight. "I will not listen to one more ridiculous word." She swivels around and kicks at the mess of thumb drives. "You're going to sort that pile by number, in two minutes or less, and there'd better not be a single one missing."

She starts the stopwatch on her phone, and we scramble to the floor, which gives me a chance to drop Mr. 421G into the pile.

"Half a minute gone . . . First minute's up. Thirty seconds."

What a team: without a word, we've got the flash drives lined up on the floor, a perfect battalion of soldiers on parade. The general comes to inspect the troops.

"Good. None missing. Now, vacate my office."

But I'm not done. "Ms. Brubaker, we can prove the mobster stuff about the Goldfarbs. In fact, that's not their real name. If you could just take a look at Mr. Goldfarb's 421G flash drive on your computer— We just need to know how many kidneys he has."

She glares at me. "Are you really this dim? Everyone has two."

"Not Louie the Lung," Tessa responds.

"Louie the Lung is a notorious gangster from Hoboken," I explain quickly. "A rival gang member shot him and shattered his kidney. They had to open him up and dig it out in chunks."

"Like picking raisins out of oatmeal cookies."

Tessa catches my frown and adds with a shrug, "I hate raisins."

"So, Ms. Brubaker, with their history, there's a good chance the Goldfarbs are the thieves."

Ms. Brubaker's face expression is hard to read. But she runs her shoe across the line until she reaches 421G, which she picks up and sticks into a port on her desktop computer. Her face shimmers with the electronic glow.

She scans through the whole medical record. "Standard stuff—high cholesterol, high blood pressure, abnormal metabolic panel. Left-brain stroke. I shouldn't be telling you any of this."

"It might as well be Swahili to us," Tessa assures her.

Suddenly, Hester Brubaker's shoulders stiffen. Her eyes go wide and her mouth turns to a huge gaping hole. "One. Mr. Goldfarb has one kidney."

Tessa jabs me in the ribs.

"This is not proof," Ms. Brubaker says sternly. "And there's an easy way to resolve any confusion. We require a fingerprint to identify each resident in case they wander away or get in an accident or . . ." She trails off. "This is irregular. Mr. Goldfarb refused to allow his fingerprints to be taken."

Tessa slides Ms. Brubaker a sly look. "Would a mobster give you his fingerprints?"

"I should have noted that before admitting him." She sinks back in her chair and seems to be talking to herself, not to us. "Our patient roster was down, and Corporate was hounding me. They're bean counters, not caregivers." She looks up sharply. "You didn't hear me say that."

"Absolutely not!" Tessa affirms.

"Me neither." I'll add it to the list of things she's said that my ears haven't heard. Man, if I were a mobster, I could blackmail her. It would be like a scholarship to college! I try to keep from sounding smug. "So, Ms. Brubaker, wouldn't you agree that the kidney and the fingerprints are proof enough? We've nailed Louie the Lung!"

I expect to see a look of shock and embarrassment on Hester Brubaker's face. Bona fide mobsters, right in her haven for seniors. The horror! But what I see instead is something more like triumph.

"It seems I misjudged you, Eddie. My apologies. I'll alert the authorities about this situation immediately. Now, OUT OF MY OFFICE."

In the hall, I whisper to Tessa, "Explain that reaction."

"She's relieved that the Silver Brook thieves have been identified?"

"Or maybe . . . relieved that they make better scapegoats than I do."

Tessa tilts her head in thought. "Wait. After all this, do you think they aren't the real thieves?"

"I'm just saying, Ms. Brubaker's been pretty eager to pin the thefts on *somebody*. Anybody. First me, and now the Goldfarbs. What if that's because . . ."

"Whoa!" Tessa gasps. "She's covering her own tracks!"

"So maybe Hester Brubaker is the thief!"

41

We scuttle down to the basement to strategize, guided by Tessa's phone flashlight so we don't break our necks. My heart's pounding clear down to my tingling fingertips.

"Theory," Tessa says. "Madame Brubaker's the plumber's accomplice. She steals the residents' stuff, then hides it down here for Plumber Matt to sneak out of Silver Brook in his handy little tool belt. That way Brubaker never gets caught in possession of stolen goods."

"So if the police find anything incriminating, she just lays the blame on the plumber."

She's frowning. "But he could just as easily snitch on her, and they'd both end up at the Oklahoma State Pen. Not the most foolproof plan."

"Which must be why she planted Thelma

Boniface's ring in my backpack. Gets them both off the hook."

"Brilliant. It all adds up."

"If we find the proof," I remind Tessa. For starters, we check the spy cam.

"Look!" Tessa gasps when we see a shadowy figure creeping toward the Ecru Enamel paint drum. But the footage is from pre-dawn and the basement's almost pitch black, so it's impossible to be sure who the sneak is. What's clear, though, is that it's not a staff member coming after supplies. No, it's a person carrying a dark drawstring pouch. Just as they start to slide Ecru Enamel aside, the cheapo camera winks and dozes off. When it tunes back in, the lean, shadowy figure is rushing up the basement steps, without the pouch.

"That's gotta be Brubaker!" Tessa whispers. "This is *it*!"

"Except there's no way to prove it's her. There's no clear view of her face in the dark."

A couple of seconds later on the sped-up footage, there's the plumber in what qualifies as daylight down here in the basement. The camera catches him pushing Ecru Enamel aside, then squatting and prying up a small, jagged block of concrete from the floor where the paint drum used to stand. He slides the piece of the floor out of the way to dig around in a hole underneath. Glancing over his shoulder to make sure no one's watching (ha!), he fishes out the drawstring pouch we saw earlier, unknots it, and pulls out a necklace of beads so white that they nearly glow in the dark.

Mrs. Dorian's pure, perfect pearls.

And the cam goes dark.

Tessa and I immediately lunge for Ecru Enamel. We manage to roll it a few inches, and there's the crack in the cement underneath. Tessa lifts it up to expose the muddy hole. Nothing in it now.

"Well," says Tessa, "this is definitely where the loot gets hidden until the plumber can come grab it. Our video evidence incriminates him, but it won't be enough to take down Brubaker—assuming you're right about her being the thief."

"Seems like it's enough to rule out the Goldfarbs, though," I point out. "It would take them about two hours to negotiate those stairs with their walkers."

Tessa twists a pink strand of hair around her finger as she thinks. "Then again, if Mr. Goldfarb can talk and pretends he can't, there's no guarantee they're not secretly doing taekwondo when no one's watching."

She's got a good point there. "They could be in on it, and they'd sure know how to fence stolen goods."

We re-cover the hole in the floor and move Ecru Enamel back into place.

"So now what?" I ask.

"We'll just have to be patient, Lewin. The thief will steal something again—it's only a matter of time. And then we'll take the video evidence to the cops."

I nod and return the camera to its spot. The best we can do is wait. Like Yogi Berra and my lawyer said: *It ain't over till it's over.*

42

I'm barely done with breakfast the next morning when Earl Archer calls me, gasping on the other end of the phone. Maybe he's having a heart attack. "Press your button! Call the nurse!" I scream into the phone.

"No, no, I'm good. Just get over here quick. Things are hopping like bunny rabbits."

I text Tessa asking her to meet me at Silver Brook, and I sprint over to wait for her. Two black cars are parked in a no-parking fire zone.

"Have I missed anything?" Tessa runs up the ramp to join me on the porch. "I just got out of the shower." Her hair hangs to her waist and looks pinker than ever when it's wet.

Inside, three FBI agents huddle with Fake-Cop Kinsey, Hester Brubaker, Detective Apodaca, and a couple of cops in bulletproof vests. Flambé sniffs the shoes of the Men in Black, probably hoping they've stepped in something gross. Ms. Brubaker says, "I was suspicious from the minute they arrived. And now it's clear they must be the thieves who've been tormenting the blessed souls here."

They all march to the Goldfarbs' room. We trail them, darting in and out of sight and advancing a few steps only when they have their backs to us.

After a thundering knock, Mrs. Goldfarb cracks the door a few inches. Her eyes blaze, her jaw drops, and she hisses over her shoulder, "Feds, Louie," as she slams the door. We hear some rushing around inside. Shredding evidence? Hiding pilfered goods?

Now Bad News Bessie throws the door open again and goes all sugary. "Welcome, gentlemen! Sorry to keep you waiting—I've been looking for my favorite pair of gold earrings, but it seems they've gone missing on me."

The FBI guys flash their IDs and squeeze into the room. One kicks the door shut behind him, so he can keep his eyes on the dangerous criminals. Even with my bat-like, supersonic hearing, I can't pick up a word, and anyway, Flambé keeps barking like a fiend.

Suddenly the door is flung open. We jump out of the way as the Goldfarbs' walkers clunk out into the hall, with one FBI guy pulling Mister and the other pulling Missus. Flambé leads the parade to the main entrance, and Lina nearly dances on the sensor to open the front door.

Mr. Goldfarb, who's handcuffed to his walker, which is handcuffed to his FBI guy on the other side, snaps, "Take it easy! We're not gonna make a break for it now."

"He can speak!" Ms. Brubaker shrieks.

"Yeah, yeah, lucky you haven't had to hear me tell you what I think of you!"

Once the Goldfarbs have been escorted off the premises, Detective Apodaca and his crew take over the investigation. They snap on plastic gloves to start the search of the Goldfarbs' apartment. Fake-Cop Kinsey says, "All you gotta do is turn up that missing merchandise, and these crooks'll have petty theft added to their rap sheet, as if bootlegging and extortion weren't enough already."

Detective Apodaca gives him a look that could peel Ecru Enamel paint off a wall. "Who are you again?"

Kinsey clears his throat. "I'm the security guard here."

"Well," the detective mutters, "seems like you've done a great job."

43

"What happens next?" I ask Detective Apodaca. "The Goldfarbs are too old to go to jail." Or maybe not, but who wants to send two ninety-something-year-olds to the slammer?

Fake-Cop Kinsey hitches up his pants. "Leavenworth Penitentiary, betcha that's where those crusty old mobsters will wind up."

Detective Apodaca gives him another snarly look. "I don't believe anybody was talking to you, my friend." He turns his attention to me. "It depends on whether we find proof that they've been stealing valuables here. Their other crimes are sixty years in the past, and if they've lived law-abiding lives since then, that's one thing. If they've been spending their golden years robbing their neighbors, that's a whole different situation. Hats off to you for bringing them to my attention, Eddie. Things wouldn't have moved so quickly if I hadn't already been looking into them when we got the call from Ms. Brubaker."

He heads into the apartment, and I pull Tessa farther down the hallway so we can talk. By now her hair has dried and frizzed up into a huge pink lion mane.

"This is bad," I whisper. "What if we helped Ms. Brubaker frame the Goldfarbs for a crime they didn't commit?"

Here's the movie in my head. Bad News Bessie's perched on her walker seat, raking and rattling her tin cup across the bars of her stony cell, and saying, "Why, look, darling, it's that nice correctional officer boy with the electrified baton!" But Louie the Lung won't hear her because he's in a different cell block, shouting, "Have moicey, I only got one kidney!"

"Look, I enjoyed the Goldfarbs as much as the next volunteer," says Tessa. "But they *did* commit a bunch of crimes, even if stealing from their fellow seniors wasn't one of them."

"But it's not fair if Ms. Brubaker is the real thief and gets away with it!"

"I know, but there's nothing we can do about that. We still don't have any proof that it's her."

I think back to what Mrs. Goldfarb said to the feds a few minutes ago. *I've been looking for my favorite pair of gold earrings . . .*

"Or do we?"

Detective Apodaca is conferring with Ms. Brubaker and the rest of the Silver Brook staff out in the lobby. I sidle up to him, with Tessa right behind me. "Excuse me, sir."

"What can I do for you, Eddie?"

"I'm just wondering if you've checked the security cameras yet."

Ms. Brubaker jumps in. "As I've told Detective Apodaca already, we don't have security cameras. We value our residents' privacy . . ."

"You do have one security camera, though," I say loudly. I gulp and swallow a wad of spit. "The one in the basement. Maybe the detective could check that one."

Ms. Brubaker looks torn between alarm and rage—and tries to hide both under her usual sugary demeanor. "I'm not sure what you're referring to, Eddie. You must be confused."

That's when Hank says, "Oh, I told you about that camera I spotted, didn't I, ma'am? I thought it was dead. It can't hurt to take a look at it."

"I know where it is, Hank," I say. "I was here the day it got installed."

Two minutes later I'm retrieving our spy cam from its perch. With Detective Apodaca hovering over my shoulder, I play twelve seconds of . . . Hester Brubaker, shoving the Ecru Enamel drum aside and dropping a pair of fancy gold earrings into a pouch in the hole.

"Well," says Detective Apodaca after he lets out a low whistle, "this is enough grounds for me to get a search warrant for Ms. Brubaker's premises."

"While you're at it, sir, check out a plumber named Matt Bowers," I say. "We think he's Ms. Brubaker's accomplice. They're the real thieves—not the Goldfarbs, and not me."

When I'm on my way out of Silver Brook, Officer Kinsey slaps me on the back, which almost sends me stumbling into the reception desk.

"So, guess everything's settled, huh? You gotta

hand it to the criminal justice system," he says, puffing up with pride. "Sorry I hassled you, kid, when all along we had genuine hardened crooks here, real pros. No hard feelings, I hope?"

All my thirteen years I've waited for this moment when I could say, "Talk to my lawyer."

44

Big news: Dad got a job, here in Oklahoma City! He's going to be supervisor of produce for a state-wide wholesaler. Overnight, he turns back into the dad we're used to: cheerful, goofy, ready for anything. Weirdly, he reminds me a little of the seniors at Silver Brook—how they can seem one way when they're bored and lonely, but then as soon as someone takes them seriously or they get interested in something, they light up like LED bulbs.

The kitchen windows are steamed. It's two hundred degrees in here, because Mom and Gabby have been churning out cookies for the kiddush luncheon after my bar mitzvah.

Mom asks, "How's the speech coming, honey?"

"Great!" I lie. In reality, I haven't made much progress beyond *I'd like to thank my parents . . . I'd like to thank Rabbi Kefler . . .* Who can concentrate on a boring speech when I'm waiting to hear the results of the police investigation? With any luck, Hester Brubaker and Matt Bowers are having their premises searched right now. Meanwhile, the Goldfarbs are cooling their heels in the county jail.

Gabby's been Googling pithy quotes to work into my speech so it'll look like I know something. She snaps off a rugged edge of a meringue cookie, and the whole thing crumbles. We go after the green crumbs like pigeons.

Her tablet is open on the counter. "Here's a good quote by that painter, van Gogh. 'Great things are done by a series of small things brought together.' Of course, van Gogh cut off his ear and died super young. So maybe take his advice with a grain of salt."

I groan. But suddenly words begin to form in the back of my mind—the kernel of the nucleus of an atom of a quark of an idea.

Mom turns toward the oven, and I'm about to pop a whole Hershey's Kiss cookie into my mouth.

"Drop it, Eddie!" Mom warns. "It's an evolutionary fact that as a mother, I have eyes on the back of my head, like the backup camera on my car." Or the spy cam.

Too late. The cookie is already down my gullet.

"I'm heading back to Silver Brook. I've got a lot of hours to make up. I need that cookie for fuel."

———

Lina clutches my arm before I'm even through the door. "The police turned the Goldfarbs' room upside down and inside out and found nothing—no jewelry or money or stolen tchotchkes." Lina kicks up her red socks, bubbling over with excitement. "But in the basement they found Mrs. Goldfarb's earrings, and when they searched Hester Brubaker's house they found Maurie Glosser's diamond tie pin, Ethylene Callahan's gold watch, those pearls what's-her-name lost, and two thousand dollars. One of those detective types in a schmancy suit is in Brubaker's office right now with the snob of a dog."

Right on cue, the office door opens. Out walks Detective Apodaca, with his arm linked through Hester Brubaker's—and she's in handcuffs! Flambé slinks at her heels, as if he's ashamed. Ms. Brubaker's head's bent so low that her chin's on her chest. When she spots me, though, she jerks her head, tosses back her hair, and spits out, "YOU!" as the detective guides her out the door.

Flambé whimpers next to Lina, who is so excited that I think she's gonna get up out of that wheelchair and hopscotch down the hall. "Brubaker, gone! Happiest day of my life, I tell you."

Braiding sections of cotton-candy hair, Tessa says, "Speculate, Lewin. Why did Madame Brubaker do it?"

"To get rich quick?"

"But what'd she need the extra money for?"

I picture the cabinets in her office. "Restarting her family's show dog empire, maybe. I bet breeding a bunch of mini Flambés isn't cheap."

"Poor Flamboozle! I wonder what will happen to him."

"And what about the Goldfarbs? Think this'll make any difference in their sentencing?"

"Aw, Lewin, you're such a softy."

45

Say a gust of wind came howling down the mountain and blew a pile of stinky cow manure into the next county—that's how it feels at Silver Brook with Ms. Brubaker gone. Roberto Montoya is our new administrator. He's younger than Dad and way cooler, with a little black fence of hair around a small, pink bald spot, and he wears a polka-dot bow tie, a different color each day.

Mrs. DiAngelo says, "He is delightfully purple and has brought new purple passion to Silver Brook."

Mr. Montoya is starting a memory care unit at Silver Brook so that residents like Lina and Mrs. DiAngelo can get special attention. He's switched things up with the kitchen staff to make the menu more exciting. He keeps the van gassed up all the time so Hank can take the seniors on outings—not just to doctor appointments but to concerts and Walmart and the flea market. Earl Archer got a private trip to the jewelry store, so he's armed and dangerous in case Mrs. Perlmuter says yes the next time he pops the question.

Also, Mr. Montoya has a deal with a preschool down the block. A bunch of three-year-olds will be swarming the halls Wednesday mornings to sing and dance and do crafts. Mr. Montoya calls it "intergenerational engagement," which is a fancy name for seniors and rug rats having a good time together. So, yeah, Silver Brook *will* be the place where OLD IS THE NEW YOUNG. I wonder if Flambé will eat the preschoolers for a morning snack.

When Hester Brubaker went to the clinker, the police took Flambé to a shelter. He whimpered and wailed all hours until they brought him back to Silver Brook and put him in Hank's care.

Tessa says, "Sweet Flamboozle is now the official mascot of the Silver Brook Pavilion!"

"He checks on each of us every morning," Lina adds. "After breakfast, unless he has something important to do, he sleeps here with me at the door."

I'll bet those fermented socks give Flambé dreams of doggie heaven.

Meanwhile Maurie and Herman go right on fighting, Mrs. Callahan has logged three visits with her psychic, and Mrs. DiAngelo didn't even realize I was gone. For her, time isn't about calendars or clocks. As soon as she spots me, she brings out her wedding album for us to thumb through. Thelma Boniface still sits in her doorway, staring into space, though the working half of her face smiles when she sees me. And Lina is still stationed at the front door, but now she wears her Red Sox cap night and day. Talking to her is the same as ever . . . except different.

On my last day at Silver Brook before my bar mitzvah, Zippy's in the building to work her magic again, with Mr. Montoya's permission. Azmara walks down the hall with her laptop open, dodging wheelchairs and walkers.

"Watch where you're going, young lady," says Herman Stark, and Maurie Glosser growls, "Aw, watch it yourself, you old codger!"

Azmara nervously runs through the final check. Zippy stays calm, though, tilted sideways on Joe's hip.

"Chill out, Azmara," Joe says. Flambé lifts a front paw to tap at Thelma Boniface's door, even though it's open. The poor lady panics a little, seeing the crowd of us, until her eyes fall on Zippy. Wheeling backward, she makes way for us to join her inside her apartment.

My heart's beating like I've just run a marathon—this is *it!*—but I keep my voice calm so I don't spook her. "Thelma, you remember Joe and Azmara and Zippy."

Zippy's soft blue eye lights come on as she skates right up to Mrs. Boniface's good side.

"I need to hang this microphone around your neck, okay, Thelma?" She nods. "Remember, call Zippy's name first, then talk slow and flat, and she'll answer." Maybe.

Mrs. Boniface rubs her thumb across the four fingers of her good hand, and her eyes slide back and forth anxiously.

Mr. Montoya comes to the rescue. "You're terrific, big-hearted engineers, but human relations? Meh. So, here's what we're going to do to make this experiment shine like the moon on a black night." He shoos all of us toward the door. "We're going to give Thelma ten minutes alone with Zippy so the two of them can get comfy together. After that, I'll invite you back in to do your techno-abracadabra."

He has to practically pry Azmara's hand off Zippy, but we surrender and head to the dayroom to wait. A bunch of the seniors are there, going over their sheet music from Mr. Caliberti's Tuesday morning class.

"Did you bring Thelma's robot friend back?" asks Mrs. Callahan. "Bless you. I think she's really going to enjoy having that cute little thing around."

"I hope so," I say, walking over to stand by her chair. "It's too bad she doesn't get any human visitors."

"It is," Mrs. Callahan agrees. "But that's beyond our control. The best we can do is look out for each other as a community."

I look at her closely, thinking of those envelopes in her apartment, addressed to Silver Brook Pavilion, and Herman Stark saying, *Ethylene Callahan, she's loaded.* "It's you, isn't it? You're the one who pays Mrs. Boniface's rent."

She holds a finger to her lips. "Quiet, child. We're about to practice this song."

Turning to the rest of the seniors, she announces, "We'll start with the chorus, and remember, singers, it's Louie, not Louis, and who the heck cares who Flossie is in the song? We're calling her Bessie, got

238

it?" Mrs. Callahan lifts her unlit cigar holder as if it's a conductor's baton. The others join in when she starts singing:

Meet me in St. Louie, Louie,
Meet me at the fair,
Don't tell me the lights are shining
Any place but there . . .

Lina, the ex-nightclub torch singer, belts out the verse:

When Louie came home to the flat,
He hung up his coat and his hat.
He gazed all around, but no wifey he found,
So he said, "Where can Bessie be at?"

A note on the table he spied.
He read it just once, then he cried.
It ran, "Louie, my dear, it's too slow for me here,
So I think I will go for a ride."

"All together now."
We're all belting out the chorus when Mr. Montoya comes to retrieve my squad. Azmara leads the

way, trotting back into Mrs. Boniface's apartment with her laptop ready for action. Grasping the remote, Joe kneels at the backup controls behind Zippy while I check Mrs. Boniface's mic.

A crooked smile creeps up the working half of her face. Her hand rests on Zippy's smooth head, and she leans forward to make eye contact with Zippy's soft blue lights. Good thing we didn't do the red E.T. heart!

And we hear, in the meekest, flattest voice: "Zippy, hello."

"HEER-OH!" Zippy replies.

The rest of us are totally silent. It's awesome in the real sense of that word. Even Mr. Montoya has tears in his eyes, but he keeps looking at his watch as though he's expecting something.

A little while later, it comes. Right after Azmara and Joe leave with Zippy, the FBI agents show up with Louie the Lung and Bad News Bessie in tow.

Lina shouts, "What are *they* doing here?"

The agent handcuffed to Mrs. Goldfarb's walker announces, "Hats off to you, Mr. Montoya, for making this possible. Folks, these two convicts are in federal custody, make no mistake about that. They're under house arrest for the remainder of their days, here at Silver Brook Pavilion."

Bad News Bessie grasps her walker so she can kick out one leg. "Look, friends, I have this lovely unremovable bracelet on my ankle. Louie too. Show them, darling."

He also flashes his ankle monitor. Glancing around, he opens his mouth full of brown teeth and says, "This ain't a bad place to hang out in for Act Three of Bessie and me's drama." He pronounces it *drommer*.

Maurie Glosser jabs Herman Stark. "Ay, Herm, it's our lucky day. Finally we got us a third for pinochle." He reaches into his pocket for a deck of cards. "Shuffle, Louie!"

46

The books lining all four walls make Rabbi Kefler's office as silent as a sound studio, but footsteps outside the office remind me that people are actually showing up for my bar mitzvah.

Dad straightens the tie that will choke me to death before we even get to the Torah service. Gabby jabs my arm and offers her usual "Knock 'em dead, sweetcakes."

Beaming, Mom yanks down my sleeves so just a sliver of white cuff shows, and she whispers in my ear, "Honey, you'll be magnificent." *Smack!* She grabs a tissue and smears lipstick off my cheek, which already feels pretty hot with excitement—or is it fear that I'll get up there and forget every single thing I've spent two years learning? I'll open my mouth and the only thing that'll pour out will be baseball stats.

My family leaves the office to commandeer the front row in the small chapel, so it's just Rabbi Kefler and me and the cavern of books.

"Speak slowly and distinctly," Rabbi advises for the thousandth time before flashing me two thumbs-up. "Showtime, Eliahu!"

He and I walk up the aisle of the chapel. My relatives are here in all shapes and sizes, and my b'nai mitzvah class occupies the back row, but only because they have to attend or else. We've invited a few of my friends and Mom's and Dad's, but who are all these other bodies? Seated on the raised bimah next to the rabbi, I squirm, realizing that all eyes are plastered on me, and that's when I notice the wheelchairs and the oxygen canisters and the folded walkers propped against the wall.

In the third row, center, sits Mrs. Callahan in her huge church-lady fruit hat. Behind her, Maurie and Herman's shoulders are turned away from each other, each with arms crossed over a yellowed prayer shawl. Looks like they've started a fight that won't get settled until "Adon Olam" is sung and we're filing out to the social hall.

Hank and a couple of his sons sit toward the back, dressed in navy-blue suits. Lupita and Clara are in the same row. Lina has brought a date, the great actor and choir director Canto Caliberti, of long and illustrious career.

Tiny Mrs. DiAngelo, all in purple, motions for me to straighten my kippah, which has migrated to my left ear. In the row behind her, I spot Thelma Boniface. And who's that next to her? Azmara, from robotics? Someone next to *her* is too short to see. I hoist myself up on the arms of the bulky chair to get a better look. Zippy! They've brought Zippy to shul!

Dad passes Mom his handkerchief to sop up her happy tears, and Gabby holds her prayer book up high in front of her eyes in a way that convinces me she definitely has a novel hidden inside it. The only ones not here are Flambé, who is holding down the fort, and Bad News Bessie and Louie the Lung, who are having the time of their lives under house arrest at Silver Brook.

My people. What a crew.

The Shabbat morning service is always about eighty hours long, but *this* morning it flits by in a flash, and I don't make so many mistakes that my family is forced to wander in the desert in disgrace for forty years.

So, it's time for the speech I've avoided and worried over for weeks. I get up and straighten my tallit,
since one side is hanging to my knees and the other
is an earmuff. I unfold the pages of my speech and
look out at the crowd of people waiting eagerly. Too
eagerly. The silence stretches out so long that Tessa
thrusts her chin forward and spreads her hands as if
to say, *Well? Go ahead already, Lewin!*

47

I lean into the microphone. "Maybe you've noticed that I'm short for my age. My great-grandpa used to say I was knee-high to a grasshopper." I see my grandma getting teary-eyed when I mention her dad, who died last year.

"But what if I got fully grown up, say six-foot-four—yeah, dream on!—and I was *still* just knee-high to a giant? That's what my Torah portion, *Sh'lach l'cha*—meaning *send forth*—is about: giants and grasshoppers. God promised the Israelites wandering in the desert that they could trust Him to make sure they wound up somewhere great when it was all over. Sort of the Disneyland of biblical times.

"So He told Moses to send scouts into Canaan to check it out, to see what they were up against in the Promised Land. The twelve tribes each sent a scout.

No, not a Boy Scout; not even an Eagle Scout." That gets a few snickers. "They were more like spies, or detectives. Two of them came back and said, yeah, there are enormous cities there and really huge guys, but the land is flowing with milk and honey and lots of fruit, like Mrs. Callahan's hat, and we can handle this, Moses. Pack up, let's go, everybody!"

I see Gabby winding her hands around each other, the *hurry-up-get-to-the-point* sign.

"Well, the other ten came back and said, 'Forget it, it's too hard. Those Canaanites are giants, and we must look like we're no bigger than grasshoppers to them. They'll stomp on us.' It made God mad that those ten spies didn't have enough faith to believe He would protect them in the Promised Land.

"But I'm not sure it was about faith. I think it was about confidence. They didn't trust *themselves* enough to think they could handle it. They saw themselves as puny grasshoppers against mighty giants. I feel that way sometimes on the baseball field, but my coach"—Joe's dad waves—"tells us we gotta try our best anyway. Maybe it's about faith *and* confidence." Several people nod. They are hanging on my words!

My eye catches Lina's before the next part. "Flash forward three thousand years from that desert in

Canaan to World War II in Europe. That same great-grandpa I mentioned—his name was Abe—he was a soldier whose squadron liberated one of the death camps in Poland. I wish I'd asked him which one before it was too late. I never really thought about it until a few weeks ago when a friend told me she was smuggled out of the Warsaw ghetto by a woman named Jadziya—someone who had awesome confidence and courage against the mighty Nazi giants. So much confidence that she risked her life to help people. And the children Jadziya helped to escape? Those rescued kids went to wherever the Promised Land was for them. Some even kept going all the way to Oklahoma."

There's another whole page of my speech, but I'm winging it now.

"So, I've figured out something while I've been hanging around with the seniors of Silver Brook Pavilion. There are lots of things I can do that I never thought I could, like move a fifty-five-gallon drum of paint, or look at the same wedding album over and over without pulling my hair out. Or really pay attention to what people are saying and not saying, and piece the different clues together till I understand more than I did before. The seniors show me that you've got to have the confidence to *believe*—maybe in God, maybe in yourself, maybe in both. Even if you can't walk on your own, or your teeth come out before you go to bed, or you have a sad story to tell, or your memory's been stolen and you can't get it back. You can't be underestimated. You can't be counted out."

My eyes roam over the congregation for a few seconds, until I find my voice again.

"A lot of you won't know what I'm talking about, but Silver Brook people, you will. This is what I've got going for me on the day of my bar mitzvah: I know that some extremely purple folks have my back, and I've got theirs. And that makes all the difference in the world. That's all. That's what I have to say."

When I sit down, there's silence, until the rabbi recovers and races through the rest of the service.

Then people shout "Mazel tov!" and sing *"Mazel tov u'siman tov u'siman tov u'mazel tov."* Mrs. Callahan and Mr. Caliberti stand up and turn around to lead the chorus. They sing at the top of their lungs and clap like I'm a rock star. As Rabbi Kefler lifts the silver wine cup for the kiddush blessing, I hear Herman's loud stage whisper: *"This* is a rabbi? He can't be more than eighteen," to which Maurie replies, "Yup, he looks more like a college kid." First time I can remember them agreeing on anything.

48

My grandparents storm me, every lady in the congregation kisses me, and all the Silver Brook wheelchairs and walkers and canes race their way into the buffet line to load up on the usual stuff: three kinds of noodle kugel (sweet, savory, and tasteless), egg salad, tuna salad, and a dead fish with an eyeball staring right at me.

I loosen the tie so I can breathe without my shirt rubbing a welt on my neck as Canto Caliberti wheels Lina over to me.

She looks me up and down and says, "Tell you the truth, I never thought you had it in you to make such a speech. Fix your tie. You spilled lemonade on it."

Ha, some things never change.

And then they do. Lina says, "Stoop down here. I have something to tell you. She's gone, Toibe is."

Oh no. More gut-wrenching stuff about Warsaw and starvation and her dead twin?

"I know she is, Lina."

"You do *not* know this. I'm telling you, the ghost of Toibe isn't there at Silver Brook anymore. *Pfft*, gone. She's stopped tormenting me."

My eyes pop wide open. With Mr. Goldfarb back at Silver Brook and talking more than ever, she must still hear his voice through the vent from time to time. But maybe it was never his voice she was really hearing.

I tap her shoulder with one finger—as much as I dare touch her. "That's terrific news, Lina."

Since I'm squatting eye level with Zippy, the robot bumps right into me with her blue eyes flashing. Lina sniffs and pulls away, and other people stand back to stare, as if Zippy has just beamed down from the Planet Zxxyx.

Maurie grumbles, "What's that bucket doing here?"

And Herman replies, "*Sha*, it's Thelma's short friend."

And in fact, Mrs. Boniface has her hand on Zippy's head, steering her toward the buffet table. Zippy won't eat much, but Joe makes up for it; his plate is a tower of food capped by a bagel, which I catch just before it hits the floor.

"Good recovery." Tessa waves a green onion under my nose. "You know, you weren't bad up there, for a notorious burglar." She stuffs the onion into my pocket like Mr. Caliberti's handkerchief. "Looking cute."

Does she mean me or the onion?

Suddenly, a voice booms over the crowd of chatter and clinking forks—Earl Archer, with his white Einstein hair trying to escape his head. Mrs. Perlmuter stands beside him in a flowing neon-green gown, looking a little like she's just dropped down from the alien planet with Zippy. She elbows Mr. Archer in the ribs when he snaps his fingers to get the rabbi's attention.

"Over here, Rebbe. Say, since there's a nice spread and rugelach and schnapps already paid for, if it isn't too much trouble, why don't you just go ahead and marry my sweetheart, Rebecca, and me?"

"Afraid I can't do that, Mr. Archer. You'll need a marriage license."

"So Hank, he'll take me to City Hall first thing Monday. Rebecca? What do you say?"

The room goes silent; all eyes fall on Mr. Archer

and Mrs. Perlmuter, who says, "We're not getting any younger. Set the date, Earlie," and Mrs. Callahan starts up the chorus again:

"*Mazel tov u'siman tov u'siman tov u'mazel tov!*" We all dance with our plates held high above our heads.

Next week, regionals in Tulsa, when Zippy goes public. After that, summer! I can already taste the first week of vacation. I'll sleep until noon and go to the arcade and play baseball and Xbox and snarf junk food and watch TV until bedtime.

The second week? Back to Silver Brook. Lina needs more baseball outings, and I want to see how things work out with Mrs. Boniface and Zippy. Besides, nobody knows more about Jewish mobsters than I do, and *somebody* has to keep an eye on Louie the Lung and Bad News Bessie. Why not me, Eddie Whatever?

Author's Note

I was a resident advisor in a college dormitory, which is like being a den mother or youth-group advisor, only you live with the people in your care. Well, things began disappearing from our dorm rooms, much as they do at Silver Brook. They were silly things: a hairbrush, one shoe, a mailbox key. Then we began to miss treasured objects, one being a very distinctive canary-yellow mohair sweater.

How creepy is this? No one *ever* saw the thief slip in or out of our rooms with stolen items, nor did we ever discover where they were stashed. Fear and mistrust sprouted like poisonous mushrooms; everyone was under suspicion. We'd pass people in the hall and wonder: Is *this* the person who crept into my room and stole my charm bracelet?

One day a girl came out of her room wearing that canary-yellow mohair sweater. "That's mine. You stole my sweater!" another resident yelled. The girl collapsed in shock, crying, "Me? I'm the thief?" Honestly, *she had no idea she'd been stealing our things*. She'd done it all in an altered state of consciousness. She was diagnosed with a condition called kleptomania, a disorder that leads people to compulsively steal often meaningless objects.

Of course, in this book the culprit is not a kleptomaniac—just a calculating thief. But the story raises questions about who's guilty and who's innocent, and how our lives are impacted by evil deeds of the present and the past. Mostly, though, my book is meant to be fun to read, so enjoy! And let me hear from you.

Acknowledgments

As I write this, we are in the midst of the coronavirus pandemic that began in 2019. As it was in my dorm and at Silver Brook, people are living through a period of fear and mistrust, but this time it's worldwide. To avoid infecting ourselves and others, we're urged to wear masks, wash our hands, not touch our faces, maintain six feet of distance between us and anyone besides those we live with, and stay home. When we must go out for essential food and medicine, we wonder: Is *this* the person who's going to infect me with the deadly disease? Is this a person I might infect?

Let's hope the pandemic has passed by the time you read this. Let's hope the human race never again faces such a devastating global crisis. One thing that sustains us through social isolation is art, whether it's in words or images, musical notes, digital memes, or any other expression of the hands, heart, and mind. So thank you to all the artists who have made this time bearable. I'm sending *Eddie Whatever* out there with hope that it will offer you a source of entertainment, escape, ideas to chew on, and a reminder that you are a gift meant to preserve the past and enrich the future of our planet.

As always, I thank the generous souls who've shepherded this novel through such perilous times. They're the people at Carolrhoda Books—especially my editor, Amy Fitzgerald—as well as my children and grandchildren and always my ever-patient husband, Tom Ruby.

About the Author

Lois Ruby is a former librarian and the author of more than twenty books for young readers. After calling Albuquerque, New Mexico, home for many years, she now lives in Cincinnati, Ohio. She shares her life with her psychologist husband, Dr. Tom Ruby, as well as their three sons and daughters-in-law and seven amazing grandchildren, who are scattered around the country.